**MonologuesToGo
Presents**

# 101 Awesome Original Monologues for 20-Somethings

MonologuesToGo
Presents

# 101 Awesome Original Monologues for 20-Somethings

**Joyce Storey & Talia Pura**

**Foreword By Michael Wilson**

ISBN: 978-0-9994895-1-2

Library of Congress Control Number: 2020923508
Joyce Storey Productions, Inc., New York, NY

Book Cover: John Scott
Book Editor: Catherine McHugh
Graphic Designer: John Scott
Cover Photo: CasarsaGuru/iStock.com


First edition

For information or for group sales contact:
info@monologuestogo.com

## PRAISE FOR

# 101 Awesome Original Monologues for 20-Somethings

*101 Awesome Original Monologues for 20-Somethings* is as good as advertised! This exceptional book is filled with first-rate monologues that are excellent for auditions or for educational purposes. Joyce and Talia have created a wide range of intriguing and layered characters, providing an exciting platform for actors to flex their creative muscles and show their range. The material opens the door for actors to shape it into their own and create their own signature styles. This kind of resource is difficult to find and serves professionals, students, and educators alike. The beginning of the book is full of wonderful advice for actors, giving them a well-thought-out road map for the industry. Kudos to Joyce and Talia for creating such an invaluable resource.

—**Elinor Renfield**, Director/Theater Educator
Broadway, Off Broadway, Regional Theater
Director, Obie Award-Winners: *Bag Lady* with Shami Chaikin; *Chucky's Hunch* with Kevin O'Connor; *Johnny Got His Gun* with Jeff Daniels
Director, Helen Hayes Award Nominee: *Passion Play* by Peter Nichols
Teaching/Directing: The New School for Drama, New York City, former Chair Graduate Directing Program; Yale University Undergraduate Theater Program; Princeton University Department of Theater & Dance; NYU Tisch School of the Arts Graduate Acting Program

\* \* \*

*101 Awesome Original Monologues for 20-Somethings* is truly an AWESOME find, and is a gift for working actors, actors in acting school, wannabe actors, acting teachers, and for any person of the human race who would like an engaging and compelling read. I found each and every monologue to be original, filled with wonderful observations of the quirkiness of human behavior. A lot of love is present in each and every monologue. Great audition material, for sure. Brava, Joyce Storey & Talia Pura!

—**Mark Levine**, Playwright/Actor's Studio Member
Co-Artistic Director: American Renaissance Theater Company/The Next Wave
Drama Specialist: Columbia University Medical Center's CARING at Columbia
Plays: *Catch A Falling Star* – produced by the Labyrinth Theater Company, starring Academy Award-winner, Sam Rockwell; produced at The Actors Studio New York, starring first Lee Richardson, then Sully Boyar, directed by Patrick O'Neal.
*Eyes Right* developed at The Actors Studio New York, directed by Peter Masterson, produced at London's Springfield Park Theatre; subsequent production at The Grace Theatre. Received a commission by Tony Award and Academy Award-winning actress, Ellen Burstyn.

\* \* \*

*101 Awesome Original Monologues for 20-Somethings* serves as a vast source of material that gives actors specific spoken text they can personally relate to. These beautifully crafted monologues provide words and thoughts to help make their acting relatable and accessible. Actors must "observe" people from an artist's perspective, noting human behavior and applying those experiences and observations to their acting work. When applied to the specific monologues in this book, those observations can serve the young actor well as he or she matures in the craft. The monologues in this book are realistic, honest, relatable, and truthful. Thanks to Joyce and Talia for providing such a necessary tool for actors.

**—Anthony Crivello**, Actor
Recipient: Tony Award, Chicago's Joseph Jefferson Award, Carbonell Award, Footlights Award; Nominations: three Joseph Jefferson Awards, two Canadian Dora Mavor Moore Awards, Los Angeles Ovation, Drama Critics, Robbie, Garland, and Friends of New York Theatre Awards.
Broadway/Off-B'Way: *Golden Boy, Kiss of the Spiderwoman* (Broadway/Toronto/West End), *Marie Christine, Evita, Les Miserables, The News, Measure For Measure, Heathers: The Musical.*
Las Vegas: *Phantom-The Las Vegas Spectacular.*
Film: *Trade, Material Girls, Texas Rangers, Independence Day, Henry Toy, The Mark, The Glass Jar,* Jane Austen's *Mafia!*
Television: *Feud: Bette and Joan, Emma's Chance, Behind The Candelabra, Seinfeld, CSI: NY, Star Trek-Voyager, Babylon 5*
Twitter: @VegasPhan, Instagram: AnthonyVCrivello, Tumbler: AnthonyVCrivello, Cameo: AnthonyCrivello, IMDB: Anthony Crivello

*  *  *

These wonderful writers, Talia Pura and Joyce Storey, have crafted an amazing gift to busy young actors, new or experienced. Kicking off with a compendium of knowledge gleaned from lives lived in show business, they proceed to offer up a smorgasbord of stories ready to be stamped with life experience and personal skills. My only addition to the advice to perfect two monologues? Keep digging, you'll find more!

—**Brent Black**, Actor
Broadway/Off-Broadway: *Mamma Mia!, Marie Christine, American Passenger, Sheba, Cairo*

* * *

I love the way this book is thought out, planned, and organized. It's smart, topical, and will be an outstanding resource for both newcomers and experienced actors alike. There's a nice selection of monologues to choose from with a wide range of comedic and dramatic characters and scenarios. "The Audition Tips" and "Biz Tips" sections are worth their weight in gold as well. Thank you, Joyce and Talia, for always putting so much of yourselves into your work. Your dedication, wealth of knowledge, and practical experience combine to make this a groundbreaking — and extremely valuable — new book for adult actors.

—**Mike Kimmel**, Actor/Writer/Acting Coach
Actor: *Treme, Zoo, Game of Silence, Distant Vision, Cold Case, In Plain Sight, Breakout Kings, The Tonight Show with Jay Leno, Buffy the Vampire Slayer, Convergence,* and *Deep in the Heart*
Author: *Scenes for Teens, Monologues for Teens, Acting Scenes for Kids and Tweens, Monologues for Kids and Tweens*

\* \* \*

*101 Awesome Original Monologues for 20-Somethings* is the perfect all-in-one book for any actor, whether you're just starting out or you need refreshing, new material! It provides expert tips and information about the business side of acting — such as what to wear at auditions, what you should bring with you at all times, how to slate, etc. — in addition to a wide variety of ORIGINAL monologues to make your own and help you nail your next audition. As actors, we're always looking for new material to master, and this book provides just that and more!

—**Nefertiti Warren**, Actor/Writer
New York Theatre: *Gypsy, Women in Heat, The School for Scandal, Son of a Preacher Man, It Happened on a Monday* and, *Sex, Relationships, And Sometimes...Love*
Commercials: "Eyewitness News," Chase, Nickelodeon, Scary Mommy
Author: *Heart of a Dream* (novel), a multitude of monologues, scenes, and webisodes

\* \* \*

Joyce Storey and Talia Pura have once again given us an excellent collection of monologues. In this new book, they have gone beyond what one would think possible. It could be two books: *Audition Tips for Actors* and *101 Awesome Original Monologues for 20-Somethings.* Each could stand on its own. While I would love to point out some of my favorites among the monologues, I prefer instead to highlight what I believe to be important about this book: Using an original monologue for auditioning makes sense.  Unless otherwise specified, too often, actors use selections from well-known plays where his/her performance is measured against the actor who first created the role. Using an original monologue means *you* are creating it; whomever is casting won't be comparing you to anyone else. Following the tips for auditioning gives you every detail needed before you actually do an audition. I would also highly recommend the book be used either as a text or supplemental to any class in acting. There are unique skills for doing a short piece. Student actors could learn so much about timing with a monologue. Teachers could make selections appropriate for the individual student's growth in skill development.  Finally, I'm wondering what else these two women can offer in the future. They seem to have hit the jackpot with this book.

—**Pat Goehe**, Professor Emeritus,
Southern Illinois University
Actress/Director/Counselor/Motivational Speaker
Numerous outstanding teaching awards including "Great Teacher" given by Alumni.
Websites:  annemariebooks.com (children's book series); patriciaclaireenterprises.com (connecting past, present and future covering multiple topics)
Works in progress: Memoir combining her professional life with her back story

*  *  *

What a fantastic book! This should be in every young actor's library.  There is a wealth of vital information on every page for all actors. The audition pieces are an absolute gold mine. I will be gifting with this treasure to several young actors I know.

—**Patti O'Berg**, Actress
Co-Founder: Theatre Works of Sarasota
Three Shakespearean productions, University of Missouri, Kansas City with Dr. McIlrath and British actor Robert Speaight
Studies: Columbia College, Kansas University, AADA in NY, Florida Studio Theatre

\* \* \*

This book has a wealth of interesting characters and situations for actors to inhabit. There is also engaging and valuable information to aid actors in their work. We know this from having used it. Thanks to Talia and Joyce for writing monologues that we have such a good time preparing and performing!

—**Amber Devlin,** Actress/Director/Theater Educator
Working for 35 years in New York City, Dallas-Fort Worth and Austin, Texas, and Santa Fe, New Mexico with her husband, Eric Devlin

—**Eric Devlin**, Actor
Met his wife, Amber, while playing Tartuffe to her Elmire in Moliere's *Tartuffe* in New York City
Performed in the plays of O'Neill, Miller, Chekhov, and especially Shakespeare
Eleven years with the Shakespeare Festival of Dallas

# DEDICATION

*To you, the actor: Follow your dreams.*

*Creativity is an innate gift that feeds the soul.*

*Use it.*

*Live it.*

*Breathe it.*

*And let your magic take you where it may.*

# TABLE OF CONTENTS

# Foreword

I fell in love with theater 50 years ago, when, at age 6, I played the title role in the school play at St. John's Lutheran. Adapted from the beloved children's story, *The Little White Rabbit Who Wanted Red Wings*, it proved to be an irresistible stage debut. As the play's hero, I was given a very satisfying arc to perform — full of real choices and surprises — and the play had magic. Real magic.

When the play was over, I longed to have something more than my white rabbit pajamas or crepe-paper wings to hold onto the memory. I felt on fire, alit by this first brush with theatrical storytelling. A secular story in which I did not play a shepherd or wise man; instead, I was — in modern dress — a little white rabbit who wanted to look/feel/be *different* than who he was. I remember wondering: How do they know what I wish? Do they know who I am? What I fear I might be?

At graduation, my preschool teacher gifted me with the Scholastic edition of *The Little White Rabbit Who Wanted Red Wings,* a very thoughtful and eye-opening gift, as it turned out. For I soon discovered in the catalogue listing of this august young people's publishing house, many books lay in wait for me. Among my treasured favorites were *Magic Made Easy, The Mystery of Dibble Hollow,* and *Movie Monsters: Monster Make-up* and *Monster Shows to Put On.* These books were the source for endless hours of summer play — and parental aggravation, I fear.

What Scholastic did not have — and I so wished it had — was *101 Awesome Original Monologues for 20-Somethings*. In this new, indispensable collection of speeches written expressly as audition material for beginning to mid-career actors, authors Joyce Storey and Talia Pura have created a treasure trove of characters and stories that offer the reader far more riches. For the young actor, this volume begins with an invaluable "how to" introduction about the acting profession that covers everything from headshots to taped auditions for film and television. Authors Storey and Pura — both working actors themselves — have written this practical advice section with the tough love that only comes from real experience and a deep love of the craft of acting. For actors who are either starting their careers or for those who are more seasoned but wish to diversify their repertoire of audition selections, this book offers an extraordinary range of attention-worthy characters in situations that are recognizable to both actor and audience.

Young actors finally have the perfect volume of speeches written with them in mind. Not only do the monologues conform to theatrical time (urgency! brevity!), but they are also the ideal showcase for a performer, as the authors know how and where to leave room for the actor's voice. More advanced actors will find in this book an abundant number of fresh, well-written monologues from which they can choose material that will both shake up their practice and wake up the audition room. I can only imagine my delight when meeting an actor for the first time in a general audition who dispenses with the overly done and too often not-realized Blanche DuBois or Troy Maxson speeches, and launches into Storey's compelling "Minimum Wage" (with its razor-sharp desperation redolent of Margie in David Lindsay-Abaire's *Good People*) or Pura's compassionate "Cop Training," a timely, dignified portrait of a young cadet questioning his or her destiny.

As a director, I would be interested to hear these speeches, and know more about the actor who sought out such new and original material.

Storey and Pura have conveniently labelled their pieces as comedic or dramatic, but wisely have left the final determination up to the actor, reflecting their desire to free the artist. In their shrewd wisdom, they know that what is funny is very often sad, and what's sad, often very funny. It all depends on how the actor builds his or her performance.  The authors innately understand that it's the *action* of the actor — what they *want*, *why* and *to whom they are speaking* — that is essential to creating theatrical truth. Sad and funny, in fact, too often pass for direction; they are really signpost substitutes reflecting dead-end navigation leading straight toward a quality performance train wreck.

That's another thing that distinguishes this book and its authors: Their characters are deeply human, captured with grace and dignity but having all of the complex emotions that come with being human: anger, love, guilt, sorrow, fear, and stubborn determination. As a director, I see in these collected stories enormous potential for an actor to realize a character with surprise, mystery and even reversal of expected circumstance, the latter being the source for many of the most moving moments I've experienced in the theater. Pura's "Cataholic" offers a tour-de-force litany of lame comic excuses for chronic tardiness. *And*, its final line reveals a person who may be struggling but is also self-aware — for whom showing up was a singular, perhaps even great, accomplishment. The last line of Pura's "Loser Boyfriend" explains the endurance of unhealthy relationships — including those with domestic violence — more incisively than reams of studies by psychologists and social workers. In Storey's "Death by Closet," we meet an alarmed and penitent pet owner who hilariously apologizes over and over for accidentally locking away her furry friend in a closet — or is the animal perhaps her only friend? Her "Diagnosis" *is* a spontaneous rant of articulate rationalizations as to why the subject cannot possibly be inflicted with the medical blow just delivered, only to end with the more rational, straightforward plea to retract this unwanted, unexpected news.

What gives these monologues their dramatic heft is that they are the stories of people who for one reason or another have been forced out of their comfort zone. As Horton Foote often said to me, "The actors have gotten too comfortable; remind them where and what makes them uncomfortable." Not overtly political, the monologues exhibit an activism and agency that we know comes hard-earned by women of the authors' generation. Given the current civil and social unrest in America, it is timely that they include pieces such as "Grenade Free Zone," "New Country," and, with its sly attack on capitalist and materialistic society, "Shopping Dilemma."

Which brings me to the last, and I think completely unintended, but no less great accomplishment of the book: Authors Storey and Pura (okay, I'd rather refer to them as Joyce and Talia). Joyce is a woman and an artist I greatly admire and a true friend. And I have gotten to "know" Talia from reading these intimate pages. They have invented 101 very short stories, which for the generalist reader offer their own delight. It's a pleasure to read these well-crafted stories by two reliable narrators, whose distinct voices are elegantly unified by a shared simple style. You may find yourself, like me, imagining what happens before and after curtains of these 101 very short one-act plays. Because as we know, there's really no such thing as a monologue — the actor is *always* in a scene of unrelenting connection (most often conflict) with someone (seen or not), so the actor must prepare the monologue for what it is: *a slice of a scene.*

To close, I'd like to share a piece of nostalgia prompted by my reading of "Audition." I am back in North Carolina, in the house where I grew up. It's Saturday night, the late 70s, and sometime after 10 p.m. Carol Burnett and Vicki Lawrence are on television singing a duet of "At the Ballet" from the recent TONY Award-winning musical, *A Chorus Line.* I have yet to see the show — I have yet to ever make a trip to New York — but I want to so badly. I think to myself, in New York, I will be happy. I will be able to be who I am.

Reading Joyce and Talia's book was for me like spending time again with Carol and Vicki — two women that showed me the destination, before I knew the way.

*— Michael Wilson*

**MICHAEL WILSON** is a Drama Desk and Outer Critics Circle Award winning stage and film director, producer, writer, and educator. On Broadway, he directed Cicely Tyson in her TONY Award-winning Best Actress performance in *The Trip to Bountiful*; Gore Vidal's *The Best Man*, starring Candice Bergen, Kerry Butler, James Earl Jones, John Larroquette, Angela Lansbury, Jefferson Mays, Eric McCormack, and Michael McKean; *Dividing the Estate,* starring Hallie Foote and Gerald McRaney; *Enchanted April,* starring Elizabeth Ashley, Jayne Atkinson, and Molly Ringwald; and *Old Acquaintance,* starring Margaret Colin, Harriet Harris, and Corey Stoll. Off Broadway, he has directed numerous premieres, including Horton Foote's acclaimed nine-hour epic, *The Orphans' Home Cycle*, and plays by Eve Ensler, Marcus Gardley, Rebecca Gilman, David Grimm, John Guare, Beth Henley, and Chris Shinn among many others. His films include the 2014 Emmy and DGA Award nominated Lifetime/Ostar television movie of *The Trip to Bountiful* and the indie film, *Showing Roots,* starring Uzo Aduba, Adam Brody, and Maggie Grace. From 1998 to 2011, he was Artistic Director of Hartford Stage, where he commissioned and developed Quiara Alegria Hudes's Pulitzer Prize-winning play *Water by the Spoonful.* He is the recipient of an Honorary Doctorate of Fine Arts from the University of Hartford and has guest lectured for the Shepherd School of Music/Opera Studies Program at Rice University; the Dramatic Writing Program at NYU's Tisch School of the Arts; the Institute for Advanced Theatre Training at Harvard; Trinity College; UConn Storrs; UMass Amherst; and the University of North Carolina at Chapel Hill, where he graduated as a Morehead-Cain Scholar in 1987.

# ACKNOWLEDGMENTS

It takes a village — it really does. We are so very grateful to our friends and family who have been incredibly supportive during the writing and production of this book. A special thanks to our husbands, Howell Binkley and William Pura, for their support, patience, and guidance. Also, to Veda Storey, Alexia Hannam, and Noelani Shore for their many reviews of the material, wise edits and undying enthusiasm for this project.

Many thanks to our wonderful editor, Catherine McHugh, who has seen this book from seed to fruition with a keen eye and strong sense of structure, message, and content. Thanks to our wonderful graphic designer, John Scott. We are fortunate to have someone of your artistic talent and ability.

Thank you to those who have built the MonologuesToGo.com brand into a thriving community: Taylor Vandick, David Hall, Molly Cameron, Umar Khokhar, Artisha Mann, Bonita Elery, Kristy Lyons, Jessie McLaren, Farhan Gillani, and RemoteLocalOffice.com, the wonderful team at Daily News Digital and, of course, our MtG writers. Special thanks to Mark Levine for seeing our potential in the early days and nurturing our growth. To Bobby Holder and the TAPNYC community, thanks for a phenomenal partnership.

To our dear friend, Mike Kimmel, who has been a guiding light throughout this and every project: Thank you for generously giving of your knowledge, time and endless support. To Elinor Renfield, Mark Levine, Anthony Crivello, Brent Black, Nefertiti Warren, Pat Goehe, Patti O'Berg, Amber Devlin and Eric Devlin, we thank you for reviewing this book and lending your kind and thoughtful words of praise.

Finally, a giant thanks to Michael Wilson: You took so much time and care in reviewing this book. Thank you for your thoughtful insights in writing the eloquent foreword. Your contribution has been invaluable and your care and love for this project can never be repaid.

# ABOUT THIS BOOK

This book is written for you. Before you walk into an audition, you must hone your craft and fill your toolbox. Monologues are wonderful mechanisms for discovery as well as necessary tools for auditions. As professional actors, writers, producers, and drama educators, we have had the advantage of being on both sides of the audition table. We know what it takes to book an acting job.

Prepare, prepare, prepare. Then put one foot in front of the other. Your dedication and perseverance will pay off. We have had many exciting opportunities in our creative careers, and we want you to have the same.

We have written about topics that interest and excite actors and audiences alike. Look for monologues that resonate with you — the ones that feel like they were written with you in mind. Enjoy exploring the layers of your chosen characters. Only you can bring them to life with your own special brand of creativity.

We wish you much success and joy in your acting journey!

With love,
Joyce & Talia

# HOW TO USE THIS BOOK

We have laid out this book to be as helpful and actor friendly as possible.

The **table of contents** is your quick reference to get an overview. Find the **title**, **type**, **length**, and **page number** of each monologue at a glance.

**Each monologue has its own individual page** for easy study, which will allow you to focus on one monologue at a time. It also allows you to have only one monologue at a time on your screen if you are reading an electronic version. Quickly glean information, focus on important aspects of character and memorize text without anything to distract your eye.

Every monologue has a suggested **gender**. These are provided as a *recommended guide* only; they are not written in stone. If you connect with a monologue that is not labeled for your gender, adapt it to your needs. These monologues are for *YOU*. If a monologue really resonates with you, it's more than likely the perfect one for you! Put your own spin on it, mold the character's story to become *your* story. If there is a reference to age within the monologue's text, you have our blessing to change the number (or gender pronoun) to make it work for you. (N*ote:* An actor should never make changes to the text without the express permission of its author/s.)

Monologues are **labeled** either **dramatic, comedic,** or **dramatic/comedic.**

If you are looking for a specific type of monologue, simply scan the table of contents. They are all labeled there for quick reference.

### *A note about the dramatic/comedic monologues:*

Some monologues may be dramatic but still have humor, while many comedic ones have poignant moments of dramatic impact. Just like life, most well-crafted monologues are inherently *dramadies.* If we felt there was a balance of both in a monologue, we labeled it *dramatic/comedic.* These selections offer a large scope of possibility in terms of your sense of humor as well as your emotional range.

### *Some monologues may have incorrect grammar, spelling, or slang.*

This is purposeful, as it is meant to convey the character's speech habits. It informs both actor and audience about the person the actor is portraying, and is meant to add interest and insight into the character. *Please note*: Some of the monologues in this book may have "colorful language." If you are uncomfortable saying any of the words in a particular monologue, please feel free to make substitutions within the context of the piece that work for you.

*There are very few stage directions in these monologues.*

This is intentional. They are designed for universal use and to allow for maximum flexibility of time and place. You, the actor, get to choose the best location and time that works for your interpretation of the role. Such choices are the foundation of an actor's performance. The more specific you are in your choices, the more they will resonate with your audience, both enriching your work and forging a deeper connection between you (the player) and your transported spectators.

*Though there are no specified accents in the stage directions for these characters, you are welcome to use an accent if it brings an added dimension to the piece.*

A cautionary note: If you choose to use an accent, make sure you work with a dialect coach to polish it. If your accent sounds phony, DO NOT use it. It will weaken your performance and distract your audience. The goal is to show your imaginative skills at revealing the often overlooked truths that make us human. So, be ruthlessly honest with yourself: **If an accent does not sound authentic, then neither will you. Better not to use it!**

# AUDITION TIPS FOR ACTORS

- Most general auditions ask for two **contrasting** monologues — one dramatic and one comedic — so it's important to be prepared with two pieces at **all times**.

- It is not uncommon to be asked to perform a **third** monologue during an audition. So, it's a good idea to have a **third** contrasting monologue prepared as well. Over time, you will build a distinctive portfolio of pieces that present you at your very best.

- Your monologues should be **well-memorized** and **rehearsed**. Until you develop your own process for developing these mini-plays — which is what the best monologues are — you may wish to work with a coach to sharpen your work. You'll know when it's right for you to fly solo at this and when, perhaps later in your career, you have reached a period where you need a coach once more. It happens to all artists. There's no shame in needing a discerning eye, fresh ears, and a guiding hand.

- Carry at least two color 8x10 headshots to all auditions. If you are auditioning regularly, always carry them with you. Place them in a folder so they don't get damaged. Headshots **always include** resumes neatly stapled to the back. Use four staples, one on each corner and trim your resume to fit your headshot.

- Dress professionally in solid colors. Wear something relatively fitted and flattering to your coloring. Blue is always a good choice. Stay away from black and white. Small patterns are not good on camera. Large jewelry detracts from your face and should be avoided. When possible, wear something that suits the character, but do not go overboard in costuming.

- As a general rule, do not use props. You can mime anything you need and if something is considered necessary, it will be provided at the audition.

- Arrive at least **10 to 15 minutes early**. You don't want the stress of being late showing in your audition. You also need to show that you are a professional.

- If possible, do not sign in until after you have read and prepared your sides. "Sides" are the script pages you will perform at the audition. Sometimes you obtain them in advance, but often they are in the waiting room when you sign in. In the case of a commercial audition, this script is called the "copy."

- Commercial copy is usually provided on a standard-size sheet of paper (8 ½ x 11) when you sign in. However, you are usually expected to read it from a handwritten poster board beside the camera in the audition. You should practice reading poster boards at home, moving your eyes between the poster board and the camera. (This is different from self-taping, where you can read from your phone, a computer screen or whatever you find most comfortable.)

- Always be courteous to the people in the waiting room. Your audition experience begins the moment you arrive.

- When entering the audition room, be pleasant and professional. Do not use this time for a lot of small talk. Say hello in an amiable manner and give the person running the audition your headshot. Do not shake hands with the audition team. Follow direction, do your work, say a polite "thank you," and leave the room.

- If you are given an adjustment in the way they want you to play the role, do not argue. They may be looking to see how much "range" you have. Take the adjustment and play the role differently.

- Practice your improvisational skills. Your ability to improv could book you the job. Only improvise when asked and always stick to the script unless told otherwise.

- If you receive a callback, wear the same thing you wore on the first audition. If they are looking for the guy in the blue shirt and you come back in a green shirt, they may not recognize you. Bring a couple of headshots to the callback just in case.

- Enjoy your audition! This is your chance to perform and show people what you can do. Remember, they want you to do well. They need to find a strong actor to play the role and it could be you! Once the audition is over, forget about it. You've done your best. The rest is out of your hands.

# BIZ TIPS

## *HEADSHOTS*

When you walk into an audition, you need to have your tools in your pocket. You MUST have an 8x10 color headshot (no one uses black-and-white anymore) that truly looks like you. You would be amazed at how many headshots do not represent the true likeness of an actor. Perhaps the person has aged or had a change of hair color or style since the shot was taken.

***When you change your look, you MUST change your headshot.***

This can get expensive, so think about that next haircut before your stylist picks up the scissors because chances are, you'll have to keep it for quite some time.

Men sometimes use a clean-shaven shot as their main shot and have a secondary shot showing a beard or stubble (or vice versa). They sometimes feature their secondary shot in a small picture on the back of their headshot in the corner of their resume.

***Choose your photographer carefully!***

Check out several photographers' portfolios before selecting the one who's right for you. The best headshot photographers are often expensive and you don't want to waste your money. You want a photographer who can capture your essence. Too many actors go to expensive photographers and come away with gorgeous pictures that simply don't look like them. This is sometimes due to inappropriate hair and/or makeup during the shoot, especially for women. Keep in mind this is not a **glamour shot**, it's a **headshot**. You are auditioning for acting roles, not fashion. It is important not to confuse the two.

A first step to finding your photographer can be to analyze other actors' headshots. Train your eye to see what you think works and what doesn't. If you see photos you like, ask those actors who took their picture. Most people will be happy to share headshot tips. Networking is a very good and important community-building tool for actors. You can learn a lot from each other.

If you have a relationship with a director, casting director or agent, you may consider asking for photographer recommendations. You might also seek their advice when it comes to choosing which take from the proof selects to be your headshot. But, **a word of caution**: There is a delicate balance between maintaining a healthy business relationship with your colleagues and becoming an annoyance to them. Producers, directors, writers, and casting directors are the gatekeepers to your career: They can open doors for you, but can also just as easily close them. By all means, nurture a good business relationship between them and yourself but be wise and savvy enough to know that these people are not — or at least very rarely are — your best friends. Be judicious about when you make requests of them **and their time**.

You want to walk into the room looking like your **calling card** — which is exactly what your headshot is. As Shakespeare wrote, "There is sense in truth and truth in virtue," so possess the good-sense, virtuous-truth to keep your headshot simple and have it be **the real you**.

Your headshot is a very efficient and effective way for you to **make a great first impression**. This picture is your introduction to some very influential and potentially impactful people in your life. Your picture needs to convey the same **professionalism that governs your devotion and discipline to the craft. A snapshot will not cut it.**

If you know a good amateur photographer who can make you look stunning, that's fine. **Just remember: The picture must be of very high quality.** You are competing in an extremely tough marketplace and, **even in this era of pervasive social media, your headshot is still your primary calling card.**

A headshot has to leap off the desk from the engulfing sea of submissions. But please avoid employing a gimmick that makes you look odd. Don't style a photo that looks posed or artificial. "Real" is in and has been since Konstantin Stanislavski and the other Russian theatre practitioners came over at the beginning of the twentieth century. **Possible exception***:* If you are a character actor who is best at selling "big and bold," then you may want to have a more theatrical headshot. Such headshots are considered to be in a special category of their own, as they are intentionally shot to target the actor toward certain **niche roles**, such as broader character parts or even stand-up. If you are using this type of shot, you may also want to have a second, more "legit-looking" photo. Actors often have more than one headshot in their arsenal. Like the right monologue, one size does not always fit all.

The most effective and time-honored way for your headshot to stand out is to portray you in a natural, open, and very relaxed way. This makes a strong first impression because it's honest. Let your headshot **reflect the essence of who are***.* You are selling yourself — your own fabulously original brew of psychology/ spirit/family of origin mess that makes you **the unique artist you are***.* That means, if you have a streak of mischievous dark humor, try that in your headshot.

**Lighting is critical**, but it need not be expensive. The best light comes from the sun, so consider shooting outdoors. If you shoot indoors and don't have access to studio lighting, grab some white poster board and use it as a "bounce" to project the natural light streaming from a window onto your face. Ideally, you want a gracious light to kiss your face and **catch the fire in your eyes**. Your eyes are the windows into your soul and, therefore, **the most critical element of your headshot.**

Your headshot should draw in the viewer, promising a great story behind the eyes: **your story.** If the picture evokes a feeling — a desire for happiness, a penchant to be broodingly sad — then it's probably a strong headshot.

## *RESUMES*

Many people are overwhelmed when it comes to creating a resume. Don't be. It's not as difficult or complicated as you might think. You can find samples online with a quick internet search.

First rule of thumb: Don't clog it up with too many words. Unlike other types of resumes, you don't use full sentences for an acting resume. Put the pertinent information in columns and use 10- or 12-point type in a simple font. Your name (in big, bold letters), contact information and union status go at the top **center**. *For safety reasons, we don't recommend including home numbers or addresses. A cell-phone number will suffice.* **If you have a manager or agent, you can use their contact information.** Below that, usually on the left-hand side, list hair color, eye color, and height.

Next comes a list of your show credits. Be honest. Casting directors and agents are seasoned professionals and have an eye for what is true and what is not. You do not want to get caught "embellishing" your resume. Credits should be listed by category as follows: THEATER, FILM, TELEVISION AND NEW MEDIA, TRAINING, SPECIAL SKILLS, and

COMMERCIALS. Under COMMERCIALS, put "Conflicts available upon request." If you have been in a major national commercial for which the casting team may recognize you and more than likely be impressed, then, of course, you should list it. Otherwise, don't list individual commercials unless you have no other credits. If you don't have credits in a certain category, such as film, leave it off your resume. Also, you may put film or television higher than theater if those are the stronger credits or if film is the major area where you are pursuing work. Theater credits usually go first in New York, whereas film and television credits take precedence in Los Angeles.

If you are auditioning for both screen and stage work, it's a good idea to have two resumes, one with the theater credits first, for when you audition for plays, and another with the screen credits first, for your auditions for film, television and new media.

Your theater and film/TV/New Media credits will look slightly different from each other. Directors want to know the name of the role you played in a theater production. If it is a classic or well-known play, they'll recognize the name. This is not the case for screen credits. They don't want to know that you played Joe or Jessica in a film they've never heard of. They want to know how large your role was. This will speak to how much experience you have on set. Everyone knows that even a small part in a play means you rehearsed a lot and showed up every night of the run to do it again;

however, in film, a one-line role means that you had no more than one day on the set of that film.

For Film:
**Lead** – the most important character; the story revolves around you
**Supporting** – important character, but the story doesn't revolve around you
**Principal** – a character with speaking lines

For TV:
**Series Regular** – one of the main characters, who is in most of the episodes
**Guest Star** – Your character is the focus of the story line of an episode. If you are in more than one episode, you list this credit as a **Recurring Guest Star**.
**Co-Star** – Your character has a small speaking role, interacting with a guest star or series regular. You may be in more than one episode, becoming a **Recurring Co-Star**, but often it is just one episode.

Generally, your contract will state what your character's classification is.

Credits are listed in three columns below each category. The first column is the project name, the second is the role or type of role, and the third is the production company. For theater, you can include the director's name, especially if it is noteworthy. In film, you include it, but for a series, you would list the production company.

**THEATER**

| | | |
|---|---|---|
| Grease | Betty Rizzo | Somewhere Theatre / Director |

**FILM**

| | | |
|---|---|---|
| Grease | Lead | Production Company / Director |

**TELEVISION AND NEW MEDIA**

| | | |
|---|---|---|
| The Story of Grease | Series Regular | Producer/ Production Company (or Network) |

If you don't have any professional credits, definitely include any student work you have done, naming the school instead of the production company or theater. If you don't have any school credits for film, but are auditioning for film, you may list films in which you were an extra, as it does show that you have some set experience. However, you will want to replace those credits as soon as possible. Start auditioning for student films or small independents or create some projects with your actor friends — anything to get some actual on-screen speaking experience. Be sure to list such projects as Independent (If there is no actual production company).

| | | |
|---|---|---|
| The Greatest Story | Lead | Independent / Chris Smith |

Once you have even a few actual credits, take those "extra" credits off your resume, even if you were "featured," a term for an extra who was seen up-close or multiple times. No one can check how "featured" you were, and the credit will still just read as being an extra or background performer.

It is important to list your training on your resume. You may do it in three columns, as you did for your credits. The first column is the kind of class it was (movement, acting, etc.) Specify if it is ongoing. The second column is the name of your teacher, and the third column is the name of the school or studio. Once you have enough credits to fill out the page, you can forgo the columns of training, and list it in a more condensed fashion.

Special skills are valuable additions to your resume. If you are skilled at something specific like a martial art or playing a musical instrument, make sure to include it on the list. If you have a driver's license, include that on your film resume, and add stick shift, if you know how to drive a manual transmission. Sometimes these skills are key to booking the job.

A resume is **always only one page long**. If you don't have many credits, try to fill the page by putting your training in columns and special skills in a vertical list. Once you have too many credits to fit on one page, keep the most important ones, and take off the less important projects. You can say (selected roles) or (selected credits) after the heading of FILM or

THEATER if you aren't including all of the credits in that category. Credits are very important, so keep as many of them on your resume as possible, and condense the space used for training and skills, by listing them on one line, rather than in columns:

TRAINING: Name of Actor's Studio (teacher's name), Name of Film School, College Degree (theater major)

SPECIAL SKILLS: Skateboarding, driver's license (manual transmission), SCUBA diver, judo (black belt,) ballroom dancer, volleyball (state champion), Languages: Spanish, Russian, Japanese. Accents: British, Eastern European, Southern U.S.

Attach the resume to the back of your headshot. Use four staples, one neatly placed in each corner. You may also use a glue stick but sometimes glue dries out over time. It is best to have your name on the front of the headshot in the bottom corner in case it becomes separated from the resume.

Trim resumes to fit the 8x10 headshot. You can place an optional small photo in the upper corner so agents can connect your face with your name while reading your credits. The most important thing is that your resume and headshot look professional, so when you walk in the door, the agent or casting director knows you are prepared and ready to book the job. Also, if you are fortunate to have representation, make sure that you list it prominently at the top.

### SLATING

**"Slating" — derived from the grey rock used for centuries to make pencils** — is an industry term used for on camera auditions. It simply means to *state* (or *slate*, as in write with a pencil) your name for the camera. This way, the people reviewing the tape will know when a new audition is beginning and, most importantly, will be able to identify you — the actor who they are — fingers crossed! — going to cast. If you are doing a film audition, this is the only time you should look directly into the camera. If you are performing a scene, you will ignore the camera and pretend it is not in the room. There is usually a "mark," an X or line made with tape where the casting director asks you to stand. You take your mark and wait to be instructed to "slate your name." You then look directly into the camera and clearly slate. This is not a time to be overtly dramatic, but it *is* a first impression, so you want to appear open, friendly and confident. You do not want to linger on the slate or make it last too long. It should be simple and to the point. You may simply say your name: "John Doe" and then move into your monologue or scene. You can also say, "I'm John Doe," or "Hi, I'm Jane Doe." Anything more than that is inappropriate unless you are self-taping for film. In that case, you might add your height and representation and confirm that you are a local hire, if appropriate. You will book the job on the merit of your audition, not your slate. Think of it as a quick introduction to the audition and then move into the work. Your audition starts when you walk into the room. Your slate allows you to get off to a good start.

Once you have slated, don't then indulge in taking a lot of prep time before commencing. Move into the monologue or scene. You should always do your prep work before entering the room. Break a leg!

## *SELF-TAPING AUDITIONS*

Theater auditions are usually in-person, at the theater, or in a rehearsal hall. You are generally not expected to memorize the scene you are given to read, particularly if you only recently booked the appointment. It's fine to hold the script and refer to it occasionally, as long as you are able to maintain your concentration.

The casting director will usually provide a reader, who will most often be seated slightly apart from the director. You can easily make eye contact with the reader, while avoiding the risky and ill-advised practice of making the director react as your scene partner. This dynamic makes most directors very uncomfortable, which is not what you want, so keep yourself within the stage space designated by the casting director.

For decades, the common practice was for actors to report to a specified location to give their screen audition — often the casting director's studio offices. More recently, even before the onslaught of the 2020

COVID-19 pandemic, it's become popular (and now necessary) for casting offices to request you tape your screen audition on your own and email it to the casting office. Given this trend, a number of filming studios have cropped up where you can pay for your audition to be professionally filmed. However, you can save yourself *a lot* of money and easily do it yourself. You don't need to invest in a lot of expensive equipment. You can film it on your smartphone.

To start, choose a quiet, well-lit place. The sound must be as clean and audible as possible. *Natural light is great.* You may also use practical fixtures such as a household lamp, overhead light or even studio lamps, if you have purchased some. Position the light source so it does not cast shadows on your face. Your face must be well lit and look natural. This is *not* the time for dramatic theatrical lighting.

Wear a solid color that brings out your natural coloring. If your shirt or sweater has a pattern, make sure it is not so busy that it distracts from your acting. Steady the camera in one position. You may use a stool, table or tripod, if desired, or ask a friend or family member to be your camera operator. The angle should be straight on from the chest up. If you need to show hands, make the angle slightly wider but not more than waist high. It's almost always better *not* to feature your hands, as they most certainly will betray the guilt of your "whirlwind of passion, making you saw the air too much" — the very opposite of Hamlet's incisive direction to his mercenary players. You want your face — not the "tempestuous torrent" of your hands — to be clearly visible.

If your camera operator is someone you trust artistically, his or her opinion may be helpful in giving you an adjustment here or there. A cautionary note, though: *You* are the actor; no one knows you better than yourself. **Listen to your inner knowingness** to guide you to your very best performance.

Remember when you *slate* your name to do so in a friendly, open manner. It should be natural and easy, like your performance.

Always rehearse your audition as if it were your most important role to date (because it may well be true!), and rehearse your piece as much as possible before filming or performing for a sea of stone-faced people in a studio. Check with the agent or casting office to find out if memorization is required.

Remember: The audition is about your *acting*, not about dramatic camera movement, histrionic staging or even how well you can memorize. Above all, make sure your delivery of the material is as natural as if you were having a *real* conversation.

**Note***:* Typically for in-person auditions for film or television, it's best to memorize the sides; however, when taping, you can use your pages for a calming reference or two. If you find you're really nervous, ask a second friend to assist by operating a laptop off camera as your very own personal teleprompter.

But even if you haven't completely memorized the material, you still must know and be thoroughly familiar with the material. Having your eyes drop too many times down to the page may cause you to lose your connection with your star-making audience.

Most actors loosen up after one or two camera rehearsals so doing several takes is fine. Use what you deem to be the very best version to send to the casting director.

And finally, remember that even if you don't book this role, **it's an incredible opportunity to perform on camera and hone your auditioning skills**. And who knows, even if the director is looking for a different type from yourself, the casting director may be so impressed with your work that he or she may call you in for upcoming projects. This is your chance to get on their radar. One good audition can lead to another.

And, sometimes, you will *book the role*, which is *soooo* exciting!

Have fun filming your auditions. With each one, you will learn how best to find grace and authority within the camera's all-seeing eye.

## CHOOSING MONOLOGUES

And now for the BIG question: "How do I choose the perfect monologue?" That's easy — and not so easy. The "right" monologue will jump out at you and will fit like it was written for you. Whether performing for a casting director, agent, acting class, church congregation, family gathering, or anyone else, the actor needs to give an honest, entertaining portrayal of the chosen character. Look for material that you relate to. Maybe you find it humorous or perhaps you have had a similar experience to the character. You want material that excites you, something you can sink your teeth into and memorize well.

A well-crafted monologue will give you, the actor, a chance to show the various "colors" of your personality. If you are using the monologue for auditioning and professional purposes, it should be one to two minutes long, which is the industry standard. Sometimes the length is specified, depending on the audition. Ideally, you will have two or three monologues of a contrasting nature prepared and ready to go at any moment. Monologues are a large part of the arsenal of "tools" every actor, no matter what age, should have prepared at all times. A carpenter would never go to at a job site without his tools, and neither should an actor.

You want to find a monologue that best brings out your personality. You need to stand out among many other actors auditioning for the same role. Casting directors and agents are looking for the person with that "special something" that will win the heart of audiences. It is important that you "become" the character you are portraying. It is not good enough to simply know the lines and recite them. You need to dig down the well and show your emotional range within the nuances of the piece. Always have a coach help you rehearse and shape your monologues. An outside eye will work with you to find the truth in the character and the levels and range of emotions.

You need to be able to drop into the character within seconds of being asked to perform it, so take time and care in rehearsal so you are well-prepared and ready. "Dropping into character" is a skill you can learn and must be able to repeat consistently. This is your time to shine, so you want to choose a monologue that helps you do exactly that.

### DRAMATIC MONOLOGUES

A strong dramatic monologue is critical to the success of an actor's audition. Select a piece that really packs a punch and makes a memorable impression. A dramatic monologue should showcase your emotional range as the character goes through the peaks and valleys of the piece. You should take your audience on a two-minute journey that has such an impact on them that they remember it and think about it long after you have left the room. Well-written dramatic monologues give actors the opportunity to delve deeply into the depths of their talents and show their unique abilities to become the characters they are portraying. A character should go through a metamorphosis or discovery. It's not enough to simply play the surface emotion of the character. If a character is angry, for example, your homework is to find out why. Finding the nuances and depths of the emotion of a character is an actor's job. Playing general anger serves neither the actor nor the material, and it certainly will not satisfy an audience. People are complex beings and an actor's performance should reflect this complexity. The higher the stakes, the better the performance. That's not to imply a performance should "appear" difficult. Raising the stakes simply means making the outcome more critical to the character. Feelings and words should float from the page organically, as though the character is having the thought for the first time.

Our well-crafted dramatic monologues provide actors with a blueprint for embarking on their characters' exciting dramatic journeys. The words will guide you as you peel away the layers of your character's rich inner life, allowing you to enjoy flexing your acting muscles. The more passionate actors are about delving into the honesty of their characters, the more likely they will be to touch their audiences and book the jobs!

## COMEDIC MONOLOGUES

The comedic monologue you select will give you an opportunity to show your lighter side as an actor. This does not mean you should take it less seriously than your dramatic work. Comedy is serious business! A comedic monologue needs to have just as much emotional depth as a dramatic one. Actors need to go on a journey with their characters and find the layers in the writing. It takes just as much work to be funny and entertaining as it does to be full of angst and dramatic tension. When looking for a comedic monologue, try to find something that calls to your personal sensibility.

We all have our own version of what tickles our funny bone. Choose something you connect with. You will save yourself and your acting coach a lot of time and soul-searching if you naturally relate to the material. You will also find you have more longevity with your comedic monologues if you genuinely find them amusing and enjoy playing the characters.

There is a wide range of material in the world of comedic monologues. Some comedy is actually very dark. If you have a flare for the dramatic and want to add another layer to your work, you might look for something a little more edgy.

Pick the brand of comedy that suits your type. A cute, girl-next-door type might want to choose a more light and airy style. Conversely, a more brooding type of guy would be better served by sticking to something that he is more likely to be cast in. Actors' material must fit like tailor-made clothing. Actors need to become the characters in comedy, just as in drama. And, as an added bonus, you get to make your audience laugh!

## *ACTING REELS*

Every actor needs a reel today. Before you get stressed out, it's not that hard to put one together. If you have great footage, that's terrific! You should market it in the best way possible. If you don't, that's okay as well. Casting directors and agents know you are building your career, but they still want to be able to see what you are all about. If you don't have a reel, don't have footage, and don't have a budget, here's what you do: Do your research on YouTube before you start and see what other people do for their reels. Then, choose some great monologues and scenes that showcase your abilities and rehearse, rehearse, rehearse. If you have actor friends who also need to build their reels, and want to do scenes with you, that's even better. Just make sure that the camera work is "all about you." If the other actor wants to use the material as well, do a take where the focus is on them and everyone will go home with a good reel. Take the time to ensure your performance is ready and polished before you tape it, or it will not be worth your time. This is a competitive business and you need to put your best foot forward.

Keep in mind that you need a piece that you can easily shoot. It can be set in your house, outdoors, or whatever the scene calls for. Try to find locations that don't require special lighting. You should have at least three pieces. Then you can literally shoot it with your iPhone and edit in iMovie. Remember, it's about your acting, not the crazy camera work. Most iPhones are great for shooting because they have a good lenses and the sound quality is acceptable. Create a "title card" with your name and contact information and place it at both the beginning and end of the reel. If you plan to upload it to YouTube, as many actors do, consider what information you want "out there." You might choose to use only an email address. Also be aware that once you upload your reel to the internet, it is unlikely it will ever be completely deleted, even if you take it down. Always show the best work first. Once you get more professional footage, put it at the beginning of your reel.

If you have a budget, there are also lots of production companies available to shoot reels at reasonable prices. Do your research and interview several before choosing one. Your reel is a very important tool for you as an actor and you need it to be the best possible quality. Spend a lot of time and thought preparing for it so you get the best possible product. If you go with a production company, you will have the luxury of other people to help guide you. However, make sure you are controlling the narrative. At the end of the day, this reel is for you, not them.

Aside from your compilation reel, you will also want to have each individual clip of your work so you can upload them to various online casting sites where they need to be separate. Sometimes you may want to include a specific clip as an addition to your audition tape because it shows a similar essence to the role you are seeking.

Your reel is a work in progress and can be updated whenever you have new work to show. Have fun making it!

### ACTORS' UNIONS — TO JOIN OR NOT TO JOIN?

Thanks to the merging of SAG and AFTRA into one union, there are now only two actor unions: SAG-AFTRA (Screen Actors Guild - American Federation of Television and Radio Artists) and AEA (Actors Equity Association). The first has jurisdiction over film, TV, radio, and multimedia, including the internet. AEA, often referred to as "Equity," covers live performance such as theatre. We, as actors, are very fortunate these unions exist. They have fought hard to increase our pay, improve working conditions and provide benefits such as health insurance and pensions. They also host many workshops, panels, and classes to help us improve our craft and function more effectively within the business of the entertainment industry.

That being said, no one was born with a union card in their hand; many 20-something actors are non-union. With the dawn of the internet, independent film, reality TV, and the explosion of grass roots work in general, there's a lot of non-union work out there. In a non-union setting, actors can learn a lot about being on a film or TV set or experience the commitment and dedication of being in a play. There is a lot of very reputable non-union work available, but because there is no union governing these opportunities, there are also many projects where the actor is not well taken care of during production. The schedule can be crazy and/or disorganized, and you may never get paid. Some projects never even get made.

Do your homework before jumping into an acting job. Your peers can help you navigate these murky waters on a project-by-project basis. Find out what other actors know about a project you are interested in. Research a production company online and through social media. If it feels sketchy, walk away. There will be other better projects.

If you want to be a professional actor, eventually you will need to join the unions. In the meantime, take on as much work as you can. Every job is a learning experience and you never know who you'll meet that might lead to your next project.

### THE DREADED DAY JOB

It's great that you have all your tools in your pocket — a fabulous headshot, a smokin' reel and at least two or three really compelling (and contrasting) monologues. You're ready to hit the pavement and rock out those auditions! The problem is rent doesn't wait for you to become famous or at least semi-famous — and even fame doesn't always pay the bills. There are many, many stories of famous actors who, for various reasons, have not been able to make ends meet. But that's not going to be your story if you are smart about taking care of business — and that includes stabilizing your income. Too many people make the mistake of getting themselves deep into debt in hopes that their lucky "break" will come and wipe out all that debt.

This is a dangerous strategy. As the bills pile up, so does your anxiety and you will bring that energy into the room when you audition. Like everyone, casting directors and agents are drawn to confidence and strength. It's hard to have either when you are desperate to book a job. The challenge of juggling life with your passion for pursuing your acting career is very real, but not insurmountable.

The famous and wise Lee Strasberg, who co-created the acclaimed Group Theatre collective with Harold Clurman and Cheryl Crawford, used to tell his students to look at their survival jobs as something that allowed them to pursue their art. Very good advice, indeed. If you look at your survival job as something that takes care of your well-being and is, therefore, a necessary piece of the puzzle, it no longer feels like a burden you have to bear. It doesn't have to be your dream job and you don't have to identify with it as though it defines who you are. *It does not.* You are an actor — not a server or a busboy or an office assistant. You are an *actor*. That being said, a survival job is a means to an end and that is extremely important. Yes, you need flexibility, but thousands of actors before you have managed to juggle the dreaded day (or night) job and still find ways to book acting jobs. You can do it, too.

You don't have to starve to be an artist and there is no shame in taking a survival job. It is a necessary stepping stone on your road to success. You just need talent, focus, ambition, and the ability to balance life and career.

Wondering what day job will work for you? Ask your actor friends what they do to solve this problem. Networking is your friend. Use your contacts. They can help you figure it out!

# 101 Awesome Original Monologues for 20-Somethings

# 22C

Male/Female
Comedic
1.5 minutes   By Joyce Storey

Hey, somebody's sitting in my seat! I'm in 22C. You know, this always happens to me on every flight! What is wrong with you people?! Didn't you learn the alphabet growing up? It's not that difficult. All you have to do is pay attention but no, you're all too busy jockeying for position with the overhead bins. Stuffing your excessively large bags in the tiniest little cubby. Honestly, how much stuff do you think you have to carry with you? Don't you have credit cards? You can buy stuff when you get there. Everyone thinks they're so entitled these days. Taking up more space than their fair share and then by the time the nice people like me come along, you have stuffed every orifice of the plane and there's no room for *my* stuff! Doesn't anybody think about their neighbor these days? Is everyone on the planet that selfish? Now you've taken my seat *and* my cubby! You ought to be ashamed of yourselves! I'm taking a video of this and, believe me, I'll post it all over social media. You'll be sorry you ever met me! Oh, now I've got your attention, huh? *Now* you've got something to say. Good. Go ahead. Right into the lens. I can't wait to hear your lame excuse. What? Behind me? What's so important behind me? See? See what? Oh. (*beat*) "C." 22C. *That's* my seat? Oh. Oops. My bad. Forget I said anything.

# A PREACHER'S WIFE

Female
Comedic
2 minutes   By Joyce Storey

I confess. I am in love with my preacher. He's not married, he has a dog that looks like him, his arms are covered in tattoos and he preaches in his bare feet. He's beyond the coolest guy I have ever met. Since he came along, I have become way religious. Like a fanatic, almost. I joined Bible study, every church group, the choir and the outreach committee. Hell, I'll sign up to be a missionary if it helps! Well, maybe not a missionary. That'll take me away from him for long periods of time and who knows who'll move in on him when I'm gone. I've gotta stay around and mark my territory. I'm just not sure how to get his attention. I tried wearing one of my sexy dresses to church. The red one with the plunging neckline that I pour myself into. Looks great with strappy heels and my Victoria's Secret push-up bra. But that didn't work. He wouldn't look at me the whole sermon. Well, I think he glanced once and I batted my false eyelashes but I used too much glue and it started irritating my eye and I had to rip it off. Man, did that hurt! I swear, I thought he blushed just for a second. But that was it. He avoided me after church. So that's why I'm here. You have got to teach me to bake. All the good stuff that smells amazing and tempts the taste buds. The best way to a man's heart is through his stomach so make me into Betty Crocker or Martha Stewart or whoever you think he'll go for. But ya gotta do it fast. I'm exhausted from all this churching and I got choir at six — and I wanna bring him a cake to win him over. I'm gonna be a preacher's wife by Sunday!

# A WOMAN'S BEST FRIEND

Female
Comedic
2 minutes   By Joyce Storey

Popcorn's ready! Mmmm, it smells so good. Like heaven in a bag. What show do you want to watch? No wait, let me guess: "The Marvelous Mrs. Maisel." I knew it! You're so predictable. Do you think people would think we suck if they knew we just sit home and watch Amazon or Netflix every Friday night? Do you think that's lame? I just can't swipe right on one more dating app. I'd rather stuff my face with popcorn and hang out in my jammies with you, than glaze over listening to some guy talk about football stats all night. Even if he *is* cute. Okay, maybe if he's *super cute* I could endure it for a couple of dates. But I mean, what's the point? Either he has an IQ of 10 and is super-hot or he looks like Duane from accounting and turns out to be a freakazoid on the first date. And not just any freakazoid. He has to be the freakazoid who forgot his wallet and promises to Venmo me later if I pay for his burger. As if I'll ever see *that* cash again. But it's worth paying just to get rid of him. Why does any guy think greasy spoons and Venmo are the way to a woman's heart? Like I'm going to swoon over him after a night like that! I bet he lives in his mother's basement and plays video games all day. Nope, that's it. I am done with men. From now on, you are the only man in my life, Rusty. You fetch, cuddle and love me for my dog treats. I'd rather have you drool all over me than some creepy nerd with a high rating on "Fortnite." Whoever said dogs are man's best friend, didn't know any women.

5

# ACCOUNTING SUPERHERO

Male
Comedic
2 minutes    By Joyce Storey

You think I dreamed of being a flat-footed stiff whose most exciting moment in life is getting a new calculator? Well, it does kinda give me a chill. It's sexy like a Steinway with its punchy click, click, click. The faster the better. I'm a speed demon! A superhero! I have a cape but I never wear it in public. Clark Kent would never tip his hand like that. He'd hide in a phone booth but these days, they're hard to find. You can't hide behind a cell phone. I'll leap tall buildings in a single bound! Well, maybe not that tall. I was never good in gym class. Heights make me projectile vomit. And I have this asthma thing, so running might be out of the question. My mom got me a puffer when I was a kid. I love my mom. That's why I still live at home — and I saved it! My first puffer. I saved all of them. I'd line them up on my bed and make capes for them, my superhero army. I liked counting them. Counting, counting, counting! I could count all day! And now I get to calculate tax! How cool is that? There's always tax reform and new laws and NEW MANUALS! I read them all. Cover to cover! Everything is numbered in order. I'm a freak for order. "Law and Order" is my favorite show. Why don't they make a TV show about tax law? They could catch the killer in section A, part 14 of the tax code. It would be great! Like nailing Capone for tax evasion! You know what? I *do* want to be a flat-footed accountant! I'm going to wear my cape to work and come out of the closet! I'm Marvin Kowalski, Superhero Accountant and I'm proud! Um, do you think I should wear a mask?

# ACROSS THE ALLEY

Male
Comedic
2 minutes    By Joyce Storey

I saw her today. She was glorious. Three o'clock on
the dot. I love a woman who's punctual, just like me.
I can't keep my eyes off of her. Milky white skin, long
luxurious fingers. I usually hate smokers, but if it
weren't for her smoking, I would never have known
her. Well, I don't actually *know* her, but I *feel* her. I sense
her every fantasy and desire. I'm sure she works in
a cubicle, like me, and uses number 10 pencils, like
me. An old-fashioned girl, she arrives early every day
to get a jump on the workload. She carefully drapes
her sweater over the back of her chair, pressed and
conveniently close in case the office air conditioning
gets too cool, but it never does. She gets her coffee.
She's a one-cup-a-day girl, unlike me, who takes a
second cup at 3 p.m. sharp. This is the moment we
share. When I'm at the coffee maker by the lone
window at the end of the hall, I can just see her velvety
arm shimmering in the sunlight from the window
across the alleyway. She's the most perfect image I
could ever dream of. I'm mad with desire. I want to
envelop her with my masculinity. She's shy; I can tell.
She always smokes alone. I'm sure she plays the piano.
Those long fingers... We'll sit in our little house in
Westchester — we'll become commuters — and she'll
play while I feed the cats after a scrumptious meal.
Then, we'll discuss politics until we retire at exactly

11 p.m. We're a perfect match. Oh, my favorite part. She butts her cigarette ever so gently onto the ledge. Then, gracefully flicks it out over the side, and alas, she's gone for another day. 3:10 on the nose. I love this woman more than life itself. Maybe one day I'll actually see her face…

# ALIEN

Male/Female
Comedic
2 minutes   By Talia Pura

You may cry; you may laugh. But I promise you — you will feel something. I, oh boy, I never actually told anyone this before. It's not the sort of thing you just blurt out at a dinner party, you know? I, okay, here goes. I think I might be an alien. No, for real! I think I may have come from another planet, or another physical sphere or something. Okay, stop laughing. I'm deadly serious. I don't know where I came from, but I do know that I don't belong here. I am not a normal human being. I never have been. Yes, I know who my parents are, and you've met my brothers and sisters, but I am not like them, not in any way at all. At first I thought maybe I was adopted, but I've seen my birth records. And then, of course, over time, I realized that my differences were much more pronounced than simply having nothing in common with my siblings. I have nothing in common with the entire human race. Now, I don't want you to feel sorry for me. I am not feeling alienated. I AM an alien. There is a difference. I just see the world entirely differently. You can't imagine. Like, like that wall over there. You see a wall, right? I see a collection of molecules, floating around in space, bouncing off of each other so fast that they appear to be a solid surface. Could I see that if I was just an actual mortal? I don't think so. And my hearing: I can hear conversations happening three tables over.

Three tables! That's extraordinary — you've got to admit. You can't hear them, right? Well, I don't want to hear them either, but I can. Just more proof that I come from outer space!

# ALWAYS ALONE

Male/Female
Dramatic
1 minute   By Talia Pura

When do I get to say that I'm okay? When am I going to feel good in my skin? Isn't this supposed to be the best time of my life? I tell you; I couldn't wait to get out of my teens. I was so relieved when I turned 20. Finally, I thought, everything is going to start falling into place. I keep thinking, this is the year I'm going to find someone to love. That's the thing with being on the spectrum. But I watch people. I try to see what's going on; how people behave. I'm really, really careful about what I say. I think I'm doing well in a conversation, and that this time, I'm going to get a date, or at least make a friend, and then, just when I'm getting ready to say something to move it forward, they turn and walk away. And that's it. I'm alone again.

# APPLE CRACK

Male/Female
Dramatic
1 minute    By Joyce Storey

Ya don't wanna help; I love ya. Ya wanna help? I still love ya. God hates the devil. It's Halloween. I don't celebrate that day. Why use my food stamps to buy candy? My kingdom for an apple. A goddamn apple. Who woulda thought somethin' so simple could make me so happy? Don't remember the last time I had fruit. Man cannot live on pizza alone! Well, I guess that's not true cuz that's what I been livin' on. That 'n' crack. Kidding! I'm kidding! Sometimes it's meth. Usually, somebody'll buy me a slice. But I'm so damn sick o' dough with cheese. Somethin' fresh they growed in the ground. That's what I want. Unless ya got crack. Kidding! Don't nobody got no sense o' humor no more? Ya really gotta lighten up. Loosen those ties people! They're cuttin' off the circulation to your brain. Ya lose enough brain cells, y'all end up like me — tradin' slices for crack, or an apple, whatever comes first.

# AUDITION

Male/Female
Comedic
2 minutes   By Talia Pura

I know how important it is for me to be absolutely cool about this. I know that if you smell fear, or desperation, I'm doomed. I'll be out of here in two minutes flat and never hear from you again. That's why I'm smiling. I'm calm, projecting an air of confidence with just the tiniest hint of "I don't give a damn." The thing is, I just know that I'd be perfect for this part. I'm an exact physical fit, but more than that, I embody everything you are looking for in this role. And as a huge bonus, I am a gem to work with. You can ask anyone who has ever directed me in another show, and they'll tell you I was the best part of their experience. Every time. Without fail, the most reliable, fun person in the room. But, serious, oh so completely serious about the work. I do my homework, I'm off-book in record time, never miss a beat. So, while I am no doubt coming across as affability itself, I am literally dying inside, I want this part so badly! If I don't get cast I, I don't know what I will do. If you don't pick me, I may be forced to give up on the world completely. I may never be able to audition again. I'll be devastated, desolate, inconsolable — utterly shattered. So, I hope you understand my position here and are planning to offer me a contract, because that is really the only way this can go down today. Thank you for listening. I, ah, I'm just going to go wait outside while you gather your thoughts and come and tell me that you've decided to give me the role. Okay?

# AUNT CINDY

Female
Dramatic
2 minutes    By Talia Pura

Why is it that every time I think I have an answer for something, I don't? I'm sorry, Aunt Cindy. Mom told me that you were depressed, and I thought that shopping would be the perfect thing to cheer you up. I thought we could try on clothes and you could buy me something — just like when I was little, right? We used to have so much fun. I know that you were not having fun this morning. So, what is bothering you? I really want to help. Life is passing you by? You're not that old. Is being married and having kids that important to you? Just cuz Mom did — I don't think that's all there is in life. And hey, it's not too late. There's always foreign adoption. It works for movie stars. You can save a baby from some poor country. I don't know how much it would cost, maybe a lot. Look, not to be mean about it, but I don't see any perfect guy hanging around waiting to marry you. Do perfect guys even exist? I hate this. Why do I have to be involved in this? I just want you to be happy, and there isn't anything I can do to introduce you to a perfect guy that wants to be a father right away. You know you're not much older than me, right? I've got all the time in the world, don't I? Am I going to be you one day? I'm having fun right now, doing everything I want to do. Am I going to wake up one morning all depressed because it's too late to have a baby and I'm tired of being alone? (*pause*) Great, now I'm depressed, too.

# BABE MAGNET

Male
Comedic
2 minutes   By Joyce Storey

So where are the babes? They said there'd be babes at this party. Lots of 'em. Come on girls, where are you? Big Daddy's here. In the house. One night only for your viewing pleasure. Feast your eyes upon the prize! I'm an overflowing mountain of sex appeal. A raging volcano of masculinity. A... I ran out of analogies, but you get the picture. The babe magnet has arrived! In the flesh. Okay, maybe it's not the hard body you were expecting. I could hit the gym once or twice. I'm planning on it, really. And I will. It's been my New Year's resolution three years running. But trust me, I'm a machine. A love-makin', heart-breakin' machine! I'm a nuclear powerhouse! Well, maybe not a powerhouse. I'm a power plant. Are they the same thing? I'm more like the steady physical incarnation of mojo. What does that even mean? I don't know. Let's go back to the babe magnet idea. That was good. Well, maybe not so much a magnet as a paperweight. I always think magnets are overrated, don't you? My mom has so many magnets on the fridge you can't get past them to find the milk. Don't judge me because I still live with my mom. She's cool. Anyway, paperweights are much more practical. Substantial. Like me. I'm a substantial guy. I got girth! What am I getting all intellectual for? It's time to par-tay! Now, bring on the babes! Is this a stag party or what? Where's the beer? Yeah! That's what I'm talkin' about. What? It's the Young Christian Men's Auxiliary League Meeting? Where's the party? Damn! Have I been punked again? Third time this year. Now, where am I going to wear my glowing underwear? What the hell — what do you guys do? Are you a fun group or what?

# BABY-PHOBIC

Male/Female
Comedic
2 minutes   By Talia Pura

My best friends just had a second baby and I don't think I can be friends with them anymore. Oh, it's not that I don't like kids. Kids are great. I might even have one of my own one day — maybe. I may just have to stop seeing them and their adorable kids because they are acting so incredibly superior. It's really starting to get to me. I mean, since when does having kids make you better than anyone who hasn't? That's just ridiculous. They are acting like just because they are managing the feeding, sleeping, and pooping schedules of their children, they have got everything figured out. Well, I knew them before they had kids, and I think they are just as screwed up as they were then — except now they have two little "mini thems" to screw up as well. Oh, sure, I guess it has matured them a bit, being parents, but I think time has managed my maturation just fine, thank you. I don't need to start taking care of a kid in order to be a grown up. I guess what's really gotten to me is that they just don't have time to hang out anymore. Everything is kids this, and kids that. Babies are like little barnacles, clinging to them every minute of the day. Gawd, get a life! I mean, they are actually choosing to stay home with them, all the time. Well fine, who needs them and their cozy little setup? Let them have each other, and their 24/7, built-in entertainment. It's great being on my own.

Free. Free to do whatever I want, whenever I want. No entanglements here. I'll just think of what I want to do now — right after just one more episode.

# BAD INK

Male/Female
Comedic
1 minute    By Joyce Storey

You gotta have the worst ink in the world. I mean, dude, what were ya thinkin'? Who was your tattoo artist, some kid from kindergarten? My Schnauzer could do a better job and he ain't that bright. I guess if you're happy that somehow makes it okay but the rest of us gotta look at it and it makes me kinda dizzy. You know, like vertigo. Does it give you a woozy feelin'? I wouldn't be surprised if it did. Did ya run outta cash or is it just supposed to stop short in the middle of whatever that mess is. Do you even know what it's supposed to be? How do you look in the mirror in the morning? What a confusing way to start the day. Starin' at that thing and wonderin' where your life took such a seriously bad turn. Maybe you could start a GoFundMe campaign and raise enough to try to fix it or something. I dunno, each to his own and not for nothin' but you are one hot mess!

# BATHROOM BREAK

Male/Female
Comedic
1 minute   By Talia Pura

What did I miss? Don't shush me! Look, I had to use the bathroom. I couldn't help that. I hate missing part of the movie. Did anybody die while I was gone? I thought I heard gunshots in the hallway. Tell me they came from the screen and not from the lobby. Okay, so nobody died, but weren't there five guys in that group when I left? Where's the fifth guy? What do you mean, it's not important? What, did he have to go to the bathroom, too? What's the big deal? What's wrong with giving me a two-second update on what happened when I was gone? I think you're just being an asshole about this. If you hadn't snuck in that rum for our drinks, I wouldn't have had to pee in the first place. I — oh jeez, I have to go again. You'd better tell me what I missed this time.

# BELMONT STAKES

Male
Dramatic
2 minutes    By Joyce Storey

Two years later I'm sittin' at Belmont outside the Arab
Prince's Barn Number 2 and I notice this thing. It's not
a big thing, but just a thing. You know - the kind that
bugs ya. Somethin' ain't right. I can smell it. And even
though I know I should keep walkin' and keep my big
nose out of it, I just gotta check it out. I mean, why does
a big-time prince with a fortune that could choke a horse
have *this* horse? I mean, he's nice enough lookin' an' all
with that thunderbolt swoosh on his nose and that thick
black mane, but any horse guy worth his salt knows this
ain't no thoroughbred. I mean, look at the slight way
that hoof toes in. It's a dead giveaway. So how did he get
into the prince's stable? And how did he even qualify
for the Belmont Stakes in the first place? I mean, it's the
Belmont Stakes! The maker of kings, the "trip" in the
Triple Crown! And you're tellin' me this sorry-ass excuse
for a racehorse qualified for *this* race? Not in a million
years. No way, José. So, I keep sniffin' around, checkin'
the stall and the bridle and I lift his hoof — and all of a
sudden, stars! Big swirlin' technicolor stars and then the
lights go out. And I wake up here, all bound and gagged
and then you come in and work me over good, and I'm
thinkin', "I shoulda walked away; I shoulda kept my
nose outta things." And now I can't feel my damn nose
and you're lookin' mad as hell, so before ya do me in or
whatever ya got planned, can ya at least tell me why ya
got such lousy taste in horses?

# BLANKIE

Male/Female
Comedic
2 minutes    By Talia Pura

Whoa, easy there. Be careful with that thing, please. You wanted to see it, so I got it out. You didn't say anything about handling it. It's very delicate. It's old and fragile. That's better. Gently, gently. Yes, in fact it does have a name. Blankie. I call it Blankie. Simple, descriptive, effective. What do you want? I named it when I was two years old. Of course, I always slept with it. That's what you do with security blankets. You sleep with them. You have to sleep with a blanket. I'd say it's pretty normal to grow attached to the blanket you've slept with your entire life. What? Now? Nooo, it's just on my bed for nostalgic reasons. That's all. Well, okay, if I've had a rough day at work, maybe. But just feel it! That texture — so soft, so reassuring. Okay, it's been washed a thousand times, but it used to be very soft. I don't have to take anti-depressives. I'd say it works very well. Didn't you ever have a security blanket? Or maybe a security stuffie? It's not that unusual. You don't have to be ashamed of it, most kids do. Well, there you go. And do you still have Mr. Dobbie? Huh, I knew it. Don't go making fun of Blankie with Mr. Dobbie sitting on your bed. Okay, in your closet, whatever. The point is that you kept him. And that's okay. I say anything that makes us feel less vulnerable in this world is a good thing. And if Mr. Dobbie gets to come out of the closet every now and then, I'd say, good for you. Why not? So, I showed you mine. Feel free to show me yours. I'll understand.

# BROMANCE

Female
Comedic
2 minutes    By Joyce Storey

Why do Barry and Ron have to talk on the phone? It's
just weird. I mean, who talks on the phone anymore?
Especially guys. That makes it extra weird. Aren't they
supposed to have a limited vocabulary and run out of
words after a while? Don't they know how to text? Did
their thumbs fall off? I can't imagine talking to Alicia
for an hour. Doesn't your ear get sweaty on the phone?
They don't even use ear buds. At least Barry doesn't. I
don't know what Ron's busy doing. They could at least
FaceTime like normal people. You would think they were
two old farts. Barry says he doesn't like to text. What
kind of a guy our age doesn't like to text? I actually think
there might be something wrong with him. Should I take
him to the doctor? But that would be weird, too. I mean,
what would I tell the doctor? My boyfriend's weird and
is there a pill for that? Honestly, this bromance has got to
stop. I think it's getting in the way of our relationship. Do
you think they spend their whole time talking about us?
Gossiping about the things we do that bug them? Do you
think they're ganging up against us? Blowing off steam
about stuff we don't even know they're upset about? I
mean, that could really, truly be bad for Barry and me.
I don't like that he talks behind my back! If he's got
something to say, he can say it to my face! Or else we're
gonna have to break up. And I don't want to break up, so
he's just going to have to choose. Me or Ron. It's come
down to that. He has to break it up with Ron or else!

# BRUNCH GONE BAD

Male/Female
Comedic
2 minutes   By Talia Pura

Mmmm, this is the best, absolute *best* Eggs Benedict I have ever tasted! The eggs are perfect, the sauce to die for. I am so glad you talked me into this brunch. I never go out for Sunday brunch. I don't want to become a cliché, but this is amazing. What do you mean, I'm already a cliché? Why would you say that? What, in your opinion, makes me a cliché? No, don't tell me you were kidding, I want to know! Is it how I dress, my speech patterns? What? I am not taking offense; I just want to know. Didn't I just say that I don't want to become a cliché? If I'm already there, I think the least you can do, as a true friend, is tell me what exactly it is about me that you think makes me a cliché! Of course, I'm upset. I think it's fair to say that you've ruined my day, maybe my entire week, if you don't explain what you meant. You think I'm overreacting? When is the last time someone told you that you're a cliché? A walking cliché! Is that what I am? You keep saying you were only kidding, but I think that anytime someone says they were only kidding it actually comes from at least a grain of truth. It's like being drunk and then using that as an excuse for saying mean things. No one says anything when they are drunk that they don't wish they could say when they were sober. So, go ahead, don't hold back. Spill it! You've already ruined this beautiful, perfect brunch, so we may as well get it all out in the open. Go for it! I'm waiting!

# CATAHOLIC

Female
Comedic
2 minutes    By Talia Pura

I am so sorry I'm late! I was planning to leave a lot earlier, I really was, but you know how it is. You try to just get one more little thing done before you leave. Well, no, no, obviously, you don't do that. You, after all, are here on time. Trying to get just one more thing done is what I do. I'm sorry, I know it's a flaw. But hey, that thing about being late as a sign of disrespect to the person you are meeting? Totally not true at all. I don't know who came up with that idea. I respect you like crazy. I do. I know how busy you are, and I really appreciate that you carved out time for coffee today. I just have so much to do all the time. Today, for example, I was about to leave the house, but my cat — why do you always give me that look when I mention my cat? I know you don't have any pets, and I respect that — but my cat is a very important part of my life. She has gotten me through some incredibly difficult times. I don't know what I would have done without her support. Of course, cats can be supportive. My cat is especially sensitive. She recognizes when I'm feeling bad, and just curls up beside me, as if to say, I'm here for you. I'll always be here for you. No, I don't think she was just looking for a warm place to crash. She actually — look, I'm not going to debate this with you. In fact, I'd rather be home with her right now. So, you can keep that sanctimonious attitude and drink your latte in peace. I'm sorry to have wasted your time today, but I just can't do this right now.

# CELL-PHONE MANAGEMENT

Male/Female
Dramatic
2 minutes   By Talia Pura

Why do you do that to me? You send me a message at the ungodly hour of 8 a.m., and tell me to call you today, if I can. You offer no details! And why a text? You never text me. I didn't even know you knew how! So what am I supposed to think? Who died? Someone must have died and you want to tell me in person. It would be a pretty horrible thing to text someone, wouldn't it? So, then I don't see the message until I get up at noon, and you won't answer your phone! Why is it so hard for you to keep your phone with you and TURN IT ON? I tried for three hours; you know? My stomach has been in a knot all day. You're giving me ulcers! I'm trying to concentrate at work and I can't eat; I can't think straight. What am I supposed to think? Obviously, you must be at the hospital, waiting for grandma to take her last breath. Or maybe, maybe Dad co-opted your phone to tell me you were sick. Of course, I tried calling him, too. What is it with you people and your cell phone management? Why can no one answer their damn phones? I should never have encouraged you to give up your land line. Land lines are essential for old people after all. I admit it, I was wrong. Okay, yes, I know, you finally did answer the phone. And don't get me wrong, I'm glad that you're both okay and no one died. I'm very relieved. I might even be able to eat today after all. But please, can you not send cryptic messages when all you want to do is hear my voice?

# CHEMO SUCKS

Male/Female
Dramatic
1 minute   By Joyce Storey

Chemo sucks. In big billboard-sized letters with flashing lights. First, they tell you you're sick; then, they make you sicker. But before they make you sick, they make you sign a mountain of papers saying you acknowledge that they may kill you. Murder by chemo. I'd really rather you sneak up behind me and push me off a bridge or something. At least I'd enjoy the view on the way down. Don't get me wrong, the nurses are amazing.  They're skilled and compassionate and generally have a sunny disposition but they spend their day poisoning people. Day-in, day-out, they hook people up to bags of toxic concoctions of chemicals and instead of getting arrested for it, we willingly hold out our arm for the needle and let them. Like lambs going to slaughter. We even wait our turn for hours at a time. And the amount of us waiting. A sea of sickness. It didn't used to be that way. Every other person didn't used to have the C-word. How screwed up is that? Honestly, there has got to be another way. There just has to.

# CLOSED FOR BUSINESS

Female
Dramatic
1.5 minutes  By Joyce Storey

What am I waiting for? Some guy to say I'm pretty and I have nice shoes and here's my number? No! I don't need anyone to tell me I'm great. I'm fine just the way I am. I have my own job, my own place and I have friends like you. So what do I need a man for? Someone who talks a good talk and says, "Oh, you're beautiful; oh, you're the best; you're the only one for me."? Let me tell you something. That guy? The one who says he'll never meet anyone else and wants to be with me for the rest of his life? He'll be fine for a while. We'll go everywhere and he'll be proud to show me off. But when it becomes real and we're buying groceries together and I'm sick with the flu and the money gets tight, you know what's going to happen? His head will turn. Oh yes, it will. There'll be some beautiful girl that he sees somewhere — on the street or in a bar or at work. And she'll look hot and he'll think she's great and she's beautiful and perfect and he'll drop me like a rock. So, don't lecture me about boyfriends. I had one. It was great and now it sucks. I want nothing to do with men. This girl is closed for business!

# COMA

Male
Dramatic
2 minutes   By Joyce Storey

What if you wake up and I can't help you? I wanna be that guy; I really do. But I don't know if I have the tools, you know? You're the one who's always been so together. You look after everything. Not me. Remember that time I broke my arm and freaked out and you stayed all calm and called 911 and all that? I mean, I can't even look after a puppy. I didn't last a day with that little guy before you had to take over. He ate every shoe in the closet, even those cute ones you paid a fortune for, and you still didn't get mad. *I* almost killed him with a chocolate bar. Who knew it's doggie kryptonite? But you rescued him just in time. If I can't take care of him, how can I look after you? I don't know the first thing about caregiving. But I love you; I really do. With every inch of my being, I love you. I would walk to the ends of the earth for you. I would do whatever you need to help, but what if I fail miserably? I will be so pathetic that you won't love me anymore. You are so much better than me in every way. You are amazing and brilliant and kind and wonderful, and I need you. I can't live without you. I don't know how. I promise you, if you get better, I will do everything to make you the happiest woman in the world. I will adore you and cherish you and bring you gifts every day. I will kiss you and hug you and tell you that you are the most amazing woman who ever lived, because you are. So, you have to wake up and get better. You just do.

# COMEDIAN

Male/Female
Dramatic
1 minute   By Talia Pura

Please don't tell me that it doesn't matter. It matters very much to me. When you tell stupid jokes and I see all the people in the room groan and turn away, I want to die of embarrassment. They are not laughing *with* you; they are laughing *at* you. You're not a comedian. You are a very nice person who could easily make friends in any room if you weren't trying to be funny. Okay, yes, you used to make me laugh, but I don't know, I guess your material just got old. Now, you just sound lame. I'm sorry, I know that's harsh, but I can't be with you anymore. I'm just not feeling it. I can't be with a laughingstock. I'm sorry, there isn't anything else to say. It's over, really over. Okay, fine, if you work up some new material, call me and we'll see.

# CONFESSION

Male/Female
Comedic
2 minutes   By Talia Pura

Forgive me Father, for I have sinned. It has been twenty-two and one-half hours since my last confession, so here I am, to unburden myself and receive absolution for my sins. I usually go to St. Michael's, not your own lovely edifice. They say that if you've seen one confessional booth, you've seen them all, but I disagree. Yours is nice, but I am rather partial to the cherrywood in St. Michael's, even though I am sure that this tapestry is all fine and good, once you get used to it. Forgive me, Father, I don't mean to be critical of your church. I hope that you won't take it personally. So, anyway, Father, after I left St. Michael's church yesterday, I went to the market to pick up a few things, and I found just the nicest, juiciest, red strawberries that you ever did see. Father? Father? Are you there, Father? Oh, for a moment there I thought you'd left, but I can still hear you breathing. So, anyway, Father, just as I was about to put the strawberry basket into my cart, I noticed that there was one berry that was starting to turn mushy. Well, Father, you know what happens if you take home one mushy berry in a basket of good ones. It starts affecting all the other berries and pretty soon you can just forget about having those berries on your ice cream, thank you very much. So, I picked out the mushy berry and changed it for a really good berry from another basket. (*beat*) Nobody saw me do it, except God. I felt terrible, but what could I do? The deed was done. I'm surprised that the cashier didn't see me blush. Thank heaven, you were here today to take my confession. I couldn't have held it in another minute.

# COP TRAINING

Male/Female
Dramatic
2 minutes   By Talia Pura

(*finishing a set of pushups*) Argh, one more… and another one… and… no, that's it, no more. (*rolls over*) Argh. I can't do this. (*stands*) No, I can. I can. I have to. (*shakes it out, starts to stretch*) I have got to pass that test. I came so close last time. I'm going to be a cop. I can do this. My dad's a police officer. He's a good cop, one of the best. I'm proud of him, sure, but I'm doing this for me. I want to be a cop, too. Yeah, I know that when I was a little kid I didn't look at my dad and say, that's what I want to do one day! It was my big brother who always wanted to be a cop like our dad. And my dad was so proud of that — I loved my big brother. When he died in that crash, my dad fell apart. Nothing was ever the same again. And me — I didn't even know who I was without him. But hey, I've figured it out. I understand now why he wanted to follow dad into the force. It's the right thing to do. It will make me feel useful, like I'm improving the world, and it kind of keeps my brother close, you know? And my dad needs me to become a cop. I admit it. That's why I'm doing it, but that's okay. There are things in life you just can't fix, no matter how badly you want to, but you can do some things to make it hurt a little less. Becoming a cop is the least I can do. I'll be a good cop — a great cop, just like my dad.

# COUCH POTATO

Male/Female
Dramatic
1 minute    By Talia Pura

When is the last time you used a skipping rope? Seriously, don't you miss it, along with all the other things you used to love doing when you were a kid? Staying in shape used to be so easy. I really enjoyed moving. All the time! I spent my childhood running and jumping, or skipping or throwing a ball. Now, staying in shape is so hard. I don't like to go to the gym. I go to work; I'm sitting at a desk. I go home, I'm sitting on the couch, watching movies, playing video games, and just sitting! What am I going to do? If I'm this out of shape now, imagine what it'll be like five years from now? Ten years! This is not good. This has got to change. I know I'm not going to a gym — that's just too hard. Maybe, maybe I should just get a skipping rope. Yeah. Start there and see where it goes.

# CRAIG VS. OMAR

Female
Dramatic
2 minutes   By Joyce Storey

How about you tell Craig that he's great and all but you just wanna be friends for a little while? And you tell Omar that this is all too sudden and you need time to process things. Which is true. I mean, it's really, really true. You have been bouncing from guy to guy to guy. Take a chill pill for a second. No buts. They are not all Prince Harry wrapped up in a bow. Most guys suck in general. I don't know what you find interesting about so many of them. You think they're all amazing and then disaster strikes on the second or third date. Like Omar. Really? Okay, he's super smokin' hot; I will give you that. And he's smart and talented and stuff. But does he have a *job*? Will he ever *get* a job? He's an *artist*. Okay, yeah, he has an exhibit at the Smithsonian but that's just a fluke. What about the next one and the next one? Why do you always go for guys who are deadbeat broke? And usually broken. I just don't get it. You are a smart girl, Rona, but when it comes to guys you have an IQ of zero. Probably less than zero, but I'm giving you the benefit of the doubt because you're my friend. Just take a minute and take a breath and decide what you really want. You're nodding *yes* but you really mean *no*. Okay, fine. Go out with Omar and have a great time but promise me you'll dump him after college. Maybe you'll be ready for Craig by then. He's kinda nerdy but you know he's gonna end up at Google or on Wall Street. He may not look good now but, trust me, in 20 years you'll thank me. In the meantime, have a good time. You're gonna anyway, so let's not lie about it.

# DEATH BY CLOSET

Female
Comedic
2 minutes    By Joyce Storey

There you are! I've been looking everywhere for you! Are you okay? I'm so sorry I locked you in the closet. You're my favorite kitty in the whole wide world. I never want to hurt you! Do you hate me? I'd probably hate you if you locked *me* up for 12 hours. I honestly didn't do it on purpose. I didn't even know you were in there. Sometimes you're too curious for your own good. What was so fascinating that you just had to go in? It's just a bunch of smelly shoes and coats, a broom and a rag or two. For cleaning. I know, I know. I haven't cleaned in a while. Who ever really wants to clean? Mom would be so embarrassed. It wasn't the way I was raised and all that. I can hear her now. It'll be our secret, okay? I'll buy you your favorite kibbles if you don't say anything. Those gross smelling ones they sell at the deli. Deal? Don't you have to pee or something? Maybe you should go do your business and then tell me what you did in there all day. There's no Wi-Fi in there or anything. Well, maybe there is. I never really tried texting in the closet. Not that Wi-Fi would do you any good since you don't have a thumb. You can't exactly text. It must be awful going through life without texting. What exactly is it you do all day? I know you nap a lot. I like a good nap myself. I can't believe I nearly did you in. Death by closet! What a terrible way to go. It would be horrible to lose you. You're my best friend in the whole world. You really get me, you know? So, despite the fact that I almost did you in, can we still be friends?

# DEPRESSED

Male/Female
Dramatic
2 minutes   By Talia Pura

So, maybe this is as good as it gets. Wow. That's depressing as hell. I mean, yes, I am depressed. Not clinically, I don't think, but sometimes just depressed, as in, this day sucks. If I could just do what I wanted to do with it, I wouldn't be depressed. I'd be hiking, or kayaking, or at least going to the gym. But I can't, because I had to go to work. I think there should be some kind of law about not needing to find a job until, I don't know, twenty-five? That seems reasonable. All student debt repayment held off, free rent, free food, and unlimited free time. I was not born to rich parents. They worked really hard for everything they ever got. They taught me to work hard, too. But sometimes, I just want life to be a little bit easier than it is. I'm not going to be this age for much longer. I want to actually enjoy life before everything falls apart. I'm supposed to be in my prime, but I'm wasting it spending eight hours a day at a job I hate. I get home and I'm too tired to do anything. This isn't what I thought life would be like. I finished college, and for what? I'd have to go to grad school if I actually wanted to work in my field. I can't add to my debt that much! As it is I may never pay it off. I just — okay, look, telling you all this isn't making me feel any better, and I can tell that now you're depressed, too. Hey, I didn't mean it. I really didn't. I feel great, work today was better than usual. Let's just order one more and enjoy the night!

# DIAGNOSIS

Male/Female
Dramatic
2 minutes   By Joyce Storey

Excuse me, I have what? No, no, no, no. You have made a mistake. People my age don't get that kind of diagnosis. You must have me mixed up with someone else. Check your chart. It's just a little nosebleed. I told my sister not to drag me to the ER but she so overreacted. There's been a mistake. I'm totally healthy. I have plans. I have airline tickets! We're going to France next month and then Italy — *Rome*. I haven't seen the Vatican or St. Peter's Basilica or the Sistine Chapel. And I hear they make the best pizza in Italy. I have things to do. I can't be sick. That's just ridiculous. I feel fine. Damn this nosebleed. What is it with all this blood? What do you mean I'm not clotting? Everyone clots. You can fix that, right? I just have to hold my head back. I've had nosebleeds before. I've had them all my life. It's no big deal, really. But can you give me another tissue? I just have to relax. Now I'm all upset. Look what you've done to me. I think I'm hyperventilating. Why did you have to give me such bad news? My birthday is next week. That's why we're going on the trip. My boyfriend (*girlfriend*) was surprising me but I found the confirmation on his (*her*) phone. How am I supposed to enjoy all that when you've got me thinking it could be my *last* birthday? That's insane. This is crazy. Yesterday I was worrying about what movie I wanted to watch and today I'm trying to find a donor who is O-positive. Tell me this is a dream. Tell me I'll wake up. Tell me anything. Just don't tell me what you just told me.

# DIET DILEMMA

Male/Female
Comedic
2 minutes    By Joyce Storey

This grain stuff tastes like it's from the broom. Honestly, how does anyone stick to a diet? I've been on mine for 10 minutes and I'm already regretting the decision. I think I'm getting lightheaded. If only I hadn't bet on it. How much money am I gonna lose if I don't lose weight? It's a lose-lose situation here. Either I lose the money or I lose the weight but live a miserable, broom-fed existence. I would throw this diet bar in the potted plant but then it'd probably die of broom inhalation and it'd be my fault and I'd lose the bet *and* the plant. I like that plant. It's the only living thing I've ever tried to raise and not killed. Let's not talk about the goldfish. That was traumatic. I probably should have fed them the grainy broom stuff. They wouldn't have fared any worse than they did in the end anyway. (*Proclaiming*) Those that come from the sea shall return to the sea! I wonder how many toilets have been burial grounds for goldfish? Mmmm, fish... I could go for some good old-fashioned fish 'n' chips. Why is it the second you go on a diet, all you can think about is eating the greasiest food ever invented? They make the best batter at the Big Oak. I mean *thee* best, hands-down! Their fried onion rings are to die for! Okay, that's it. Diet's over. I'm going to the Big Oak and I'm going to gorge myself and enjoy my life. What if I get hit by a bus tomorrow? What would I have accomplished in my life? Made myself miserable eating broom straw? Uh-uh. Not for me. I want to LIVE! I might be the Good Year Blimp, but I'll be the happiest blimp you ever met!

# DON'T BOTHER NOBODY

Male/Female
Dramatic
1 minute   By Joyce Storey

You're bleedin' profusely. Somebody call 911! What were you thinkin'? I specifically said to you, "Don't bother people cuz you never know when somebody gonna see you." You just had to mess with his head, didn't you? Look at you, girl. Lyin' here all banged up. What if nobody found you? You're all messed up. Leave people alone. Nobody's botherin' you, don't bother them. If your friend got a problem with somebody, that's your friend's business. You're lookin' at me, but you're not listenin'. You don't ever listen. Goin' off half-cocked — that's just stupid. How did ya think he was gonna react? O' course they came atchu. This is one bad dude. I mean *bad*. You can't save everyone, baby. You be all love 'n' light 'n' stuff, but you gotta pick your battles and this was *not* your battle. Don't bother nobody, ya hear me? NOBODY. Where the *hell* is that ambulance?

# DREAMS

Female
Dramatic
2 minutes    By Joyce Storey

When you like somebody you want to see their dreams come true. You just stand there and you can't help it. It's feeling their feelings and you just do. Know what I mean? Take you, for example, I know that you want to be a skydiver but you can't ever be that because of your vertigo. That really sucks and it makes me feel bad for you. And it kinda makes my stomach turn when I think of vertigo. I don't know how you deal with that. It must be awful to want something so bad and know you can never have it. I used to want to skydive. Not professionally like you or anything, but I wanted to try it just once. I even signed up, but then the wind was bad and they had to cancel. And then, I don't know, I just lost my nerve. I do that a lot. Do you ever feel like that? Too afraid to try something? I feel like that all the time. I can't tell you the amount of parties I've been invited to that I've just said I was busy when I wasn't, all because I had so much anxiety about going. What if no one talked to me? I can picture myself sitting there in the corner not knowing where to look and getting out my phone and acting all busy like I'm talking to someone or something, just waiting long enough to leave. Oh, I get a knot in my stomach just thinking about it. I hate being like that. Afraid of my own shadow. I dream of the day when I'll feel confident and interesting. But that's small stuff compared to you. I feel terrible for you; I really do. Is there anything else you dream about doing? Something that would make you happy? Anything at all?

# DUMPED

Male/Female
Dramatic
1.5 minutes   By Talia Pura

How can I be funny at a time like this? You expect me to tell some stupid joke, and make everyone laugh, but I don't feel funny right now, okay? It just doesn't work that way. I know, you are paying me a lot of money to come up with the funny lines, but right now is not a good time for me, you know? You think you are in a secure relationship and then one morning you wake up to no one sleeping on the pillow beside you, with a note propped up where a head should be. A note! Who breaks up like that? Last night we were doing it for half an hour, at least! I had no clue that it was for the last time! Wow, the last time? That's a punch in the gut. I didn't think I was that bad in bed! I mean, yes, one can always improve, but really, to break up, with a note, over that? Okay, so the note didn't actually talk about last night. There were supposedly other reasons, lots and lots of other reasons. Reasons so ludicrous they are laughable. Whew — okay, I can do this. I can dig deep down into the pain and turn this into comedy gold. All right people, we are on! Come on, now, we've got a show to put out!

# EMOJI CONFUSION

Male/Female
Comedic
2 minutes    By Joyce Storey

Vinny texted me a happy face. But then Jared texted that it was a sad face. And then Elise texted and she thinks it's a happy *and* sad face. That's like, impossible, right? What do you think? (*shows text*) Happy, right? I mean, when I'm right, I'm right, right? Unless he meant for it to be sad but accidentally sent happy. And Elise is kinda touchy-feely and maybe she was picking up on his energy or something. A person could send a happy face but really they're sad — but you think they're happy but then you look and realize it's a sad face so they're sad but then they're probably happy again by the time you figure it out, so you don't have time to get back to them before they change the face anyway. Especially if they're a fast texter; know what I mean? Oh, wait, look! It *was* sad but now it's happy! It's all because Missy got her arm completely out of her shoulder straps in her car seat. Can you believe it? That kid! She's getting so big! And we all missed it because we were busy deciding whether it was a happy face or a sad face that Vinny sent. And we still don't know. Why didn't he just send a video? It's so much easier. He could just Snapchat or something. I mean, by the time we got it all sorted out, Missy is back in her shoulder straps and now everything's fine. And there's nothing on video! We can't even post it, cuz there's nothing to post! And it would have been so cute and adorable! Honestly, I can't believe Vinny, can you? And why is he texting when he's driving anyway? He should keep his eyes on the road!

# EXPIRED

Female
Dramatic
2 minutes    By Joyce Storey

This chocolate bar tastes like expired sawdust. Must be sugar-free. Why is everything good in life bad for you? Like you? You are the worst thing for me and I know it. *I know it.* If I stick with you, I won't amount to anything. I was smart, you know. Could've gone to college, but I chose you. You take me places I have no business going, yet I go willingly. I leave and you suck me back in. Bad boys look so cool up on stage wailing on their guitars. But then I get you home and look at you: a strung-out mess, lying on the couch playing Wii or Nintendo or whatever isn't buried under beer cans and coke lines. Our apartment's a post-apocalyptic mess. It'll take six garbage bags to shovel away last night's party. And will you please stop vaping? I'll buy you a pack of cigarettes if you'll just stop already. If you ever bothered watching the news you'd know how bad it is for you. Listen to me lecturing you, when I should be lecturing myself. You're gonna put yourself in the grave before you're 35 and I'll probably be right in there with you, so they'd better dig a double-wide. We gotta clean up our act, Nick. Will you stop with the PlayStation long enough to have a conversation? Can you even hear me? Do you *want* to hear me? What the hell am I doing? I'm in love with a zombie. That's it. When I'm done cleaning up the apartment, I'm gonna clean up myself. And you and your electronics will have to move in with Joey or Izzy or whoever the hell you can mooch off of because I'm spring cleaning — and you are the first thing I'm throwing out.

# EXPRESS TRAIN TO NOWHERE

Male/Female
Dramatic
2 minutes    By Joyce Storey

I'm on the express train to nowhere and I just want to get off. I mean, really, how long am I supposed to keep trying? At anything. Everything I touch turns to crap. I was supposed to be an influencer by now. Have enough money to sit with my laptop in Tahiti and laugh at all those poor suckers still slugging out a 9-to-5 or, more realistically, 9-to-7. Well, who's laughing now? Those poor suckers are at the wine bar numbing out their mundane existence but at least they can pay the bar tab and some of them have probably booked their vacation to Tahiti this year. They'll be moaning over their sunburn while I'll be nowhere. Nobody going nowhere but down. I'm in debt so far that I'll never dig out. My landlord just tossed me out of my apartment and I just used my last buck on Venmo for this cup of coffee. So don't patronize me, please. I've had about enough of people selling me their personal brand of B.S. I've vlogged, I've blogged, I've done podcasts and YouTube and Twitter and Instagram, Snapchat, LinkedIn. All that crap. And tonight I'll sleep in my car. Until they repo that, too. So, don't you dare start in on me. I have worked my butt off and it's gotten me exactly nowhere. I want to crawl through a sewer hole and die. It's easier than all this. What's it all for, anyway? We spend our lives trying to accumulate stuff, and wealth to buy more stuff. Then we get old and die and can't take any of it with us. So, what was it all about? Just get me off this freight train and find me a sewer. I'm the laughingstock of my own life and I don't want to play anymore.

# FAMILY DINNER

Male/Female
Dramatic
2 minutes   By Talia Pura

Look, I'm sorry. I should have told you earlier. I know I should have, but I knew when I did, it would be a huge fight. Yes, I would call this a fight. It went beyond a discussion about 10 minutes ago. I want to go to my parents' house. They are expecting us. I promise it will be okay this time. Hey, come on. No one can hold a grudge forever. I'm sure my mom has gotten over it. Look, she was the one who actually called and invited us. She wants you there. No, not just to give you a hard time about how you dress, or the fact that you never want kids. She knows that I never did, either. She has totally given up on me finding someone to talk me out of that. She knows it is not my problem that she will never become a grandmother. It's on her, really, for only having one child. She never had a backup plan. See, we are on the same side. And this time, no matter what she says, I will support you. I promise. Yes, I realize that I promised that last time, but she caught me off guard. I wasn't prepared. This time will be different. It will. Come on, I'm really hungry. Can we just go now, please? Her dinner is already on the table and you didn't make anything for us, so — no, I know, of course, I could have made dinner for us, but I thought we were going to my parents! For Christ's sake, can we just go, please? Look, if you are miserable, we'll eat and run, okay? That is a promise I can keep.

# FINAL PAPER

Male/Female
Dramatic
1 minute   By Talia Pura

It's almost done. The last paper of the last course. No more classes, no more research, no more studying! This is it! This one little paper and I am done! Yes, I was accepted to grad school. Don't you think I know that? Can you not give me this one little moment of pure, unadulterated joy? I've worked hard, I deserve a break, don't I? I want to completely and totally forget about school until the minute I prep for grad school in the fall. Is that too much to ask? Why do I feel like you are always lurking around, waiting to spoil my good mood? Yes, our apartment is small, but there are other places you could be. You don't have to be this close to me. Thank you. I appreciate it. Just think: Only three or four more years and we'll each be able to afford our own places.

# FIRED

Male/Female
Dramatic
2 minutes   By Joyce Storey

You know, Rand, I couldn't help but feel this guilty pleasure when I found out you'd gotten yourself fired. Actually, it was more like sheer glee. You have been trying to get *me* fired for months! Don't deny it. You know it's true. All because you thought you deserved that corner desk more than me. You stabbed me in the back over a *cubicle*. What kind of perceived status did you think it would give you? You'd be closer to the coffee pot so you could get the jitters faster. Like that's a good thing. If caffeine was your motivation, I could have bought you a Keurig. Did you really have to lie to management? I'm on probation because of you. I'm a damn Harvard grad and I've been written up three times! I never thought you'd stoop that low, but I'll give you this: You'rc a really good spin doctor. By the time you're done with people, no one knows the truth. But I do. (*pause*) Stop it. The gloves are off, so stop playing. You know what you did, and so do I. Is manipulation your special gift in life? The only thing you have to offer? You swapped those files and tanked the account to steal it away from me. The Larson account was mine. I don't care who you golf with on the weekends. I landed it, not you. And now that you're gone, it'll be mine again. Mark my words. Now I know how to play hardball, thanks to you, and I will not be broadsided again. Oh, and you know that file they found on your desk? The one that got you fired? Wonder how it got there? Turns out I learned a lot from you. Thanks.

# FRIENDLY'S

Male/Female
Comedic
2 minutes    By Joyce Storey

Did you know that Friendly's offers "Delicious Beginnings and Happy Endings"? Their unfortunate slogan is written right on the back of their menu by the desserts. By the time I got to "warm gooey super melts," I had to stop reading because I was blushing so much. Hasn't their marketing department ever heard of those sleezy massage parlors? Apparently, they're a family restaurant with a very adult menu. Dare I ask what you can order on the side?! Yikes! Obviously, they're more friendly at Friendly's than I thought! Maybe they have a massage parlor in the back? I wonder what you could get "to go" if you asked the right questions? Or maybe my mind is in the gutter and I should just take it at face value? But really, just reading their menu is a sexual fantasy in Technicolor. They have all sorts of fun things: Rocky Is Tasty, Forbidden Fudge Brownie — let's not even go there — Double Thick Milkshakes, Hunka Chunka PB Fudge, and my favorite: Giant Crowd Pleaser, or the good ole-fashioned Royal Banana Split. You can get all sorts of things between your delicious beginning and your happy ending. I think they must have been reveling on a particularly good sugar high the day they approved their menu — or maybe they just wanted to amuse the adults while the kids fight over the balloons. A sugar high is supposed to fire off the same endorphins that you get during sex, so maybe they're not really off the mark. I've never heard so many people openly discussing happy endings before. Maybe Friendly's has started its own sexual revolution. They really sum it up best themselves when they say: *Proving once again that such back-to-back happiness can only happen at Friendly's!*

# GET A HOBBY

Male/Female
Comedic
2 minutes   By Talia Pura

This is so relaxing. Whoever said that 45 minutes of creative work can change your life was so right. There is nothing like the feel of clay oozing through your fingers. An hour ago, I was all wound up from a hard shift at work. Traffic was horrendous, the weather just awful. But, now, all that is behind me. All that is irrelevant. My pulse rate is down, my breathing is steady, and I am at peace with the world. I am a Zen master. There is nothing I cannot do. Well, except for getting the ears right on this cat sculpture. Who knew that cat ears would be so difficult to render in clay? Maybe if I just pinch the edges a little bit more. Maybe just — no, that looks worse. No big deal, the ears aren't all that important. Who am I kidding? This doesn't even look like a cat. The ears are everything! If you don't get the ears right, it looks like a rat. I am not wasting my leisure time recreating the image of a rat, damn it! I want to make a cat! Is that so much to ask? Could I please just get these lousy ears right and finish this damn cat statue already? This is turning into a bloody waste of time. Why did I think I could be a sculptor? What am I going to do with this rat cat anyway? Who wants something this ugly in their home? I don't, and I can't give it away! Argh, I feel so tense. My hands are all dried out from handling clay for an hour. This clearly is no longer working. This is no way to relax. How can I relax with that ugly animal staring at me? I've got to find a new way to unwind. Scream therapy might be the way to go. Aaaarrrggghhhhh!

# GRENADE-FREE ZONE

Male/Female
Comedic
1.5 minutes   By Joyce Storey

Did you know that in Alamosa, Colorado, it is illegal to throw grenades at passing cars? Yup, it's an actual law. I'm not sure if the same holds true for throwing them at people, but where cars are concerned, the fine lawmakers of Alamosa have spoken. I think I may pack up my family and move there! I'd feel better knowing my Ford Escalade is in safe hands. Or do you think an Escalade rates as a truck and is therefore exempt from the law? Maybe I should trade it in for a Honda Accord. At any rate, there'll be no grenade throwin' in Alamosa anytime soon! No sir. Not even on special occasions like the Fourth of July, though it would make a heck of firecracker. Now, all you grenade throwers might think it's unconstitutional in the land of the free and the home of the brave. What's a little grenade throwin' among friends, right?? Well, the people of Alamosa don't care what you think about the right to bear arms — or blow up arms in this case. So, while I'm busy packing up my things, you might as well decide what other state you want to throw your grenades in, cuz Alamosa is closed!

# HALF-EMPTY

Male/Female
Dramatic/Comedic
2 minutes   By Talia Pura

Did you ever have one of those days when you just feel like everything is right? Everything is just exactly what it's supposed to be? The job is actually satisfying, the relationship — perfect. Parents are largely off my back, I'm healthy, I'm happy, I'm… I'm really okay! I feel great. I know that I have to enjoy this feeling, because you just never know if it's going to last. In fact, I'm pretty sure it isn't. At heart, I'm not even a glass-half-empty kind of person. My glass is usually cracked and leaking. Like, yes, my relationship is good, very good. I think I've found the person that I'm going to be with forever. We are so in sync that last night I said those three little words that you have to be so extremely careful with. Simple. I didn't plan it. In fact, I had planned to wait at least another month until I said them, but, they just spilled out. I didn't get any kind of freak out in response, just, kind of a smile. A nice warm smile. It felt so good. (*beat*) Oh, gawd! I didn't get an "I Love You" back! How did I not notice that? How did I think that a smile was a response? I am dead. This relationship is doomed. I've ruined it. How could I have done that? Should I call and try to walk it back? Should I pretend it never happened? Should I ask if the feeling is mutual? Oh, gawd! My stomach is in knots. I think I may throw up. I feel, okay — I now feel pretty normal. Wow, feeling great is highly overrated. Doesn't everyone need something to worry about at all times?

# HANDBAG ENVY

Female
Comedic
2 minutes   By Talia Pura

I just found the perfect handbag. I know that is hard to believe. There is no such thing as a perfect purse, right? If there was, I wouldn't have a closet full of rejects. You know how this goes — you find the perfect bag, caress it, take it home, use it once or twice and its flaws start to appear. Take this one leather bag that I thought I'd adored: butter-soft leather, leopard print interior, perfect size, handle just the right length. I paid too much but was sure it was worth it. I used it once. Once! The bag was the perfect size, yes, but its mouth was narrower than its base! I had to squish things through this tiny opening to get to the roomy interior. Such a disappointment. But, oh, this bag — this is the bag of my dreams. I can now open my closet door and say sayonara to that pile of trash. This is the only bag I'll ever use. It's not only the perfect size with an ample opening, it's also a fabulous color. The only problem is, I don't know where to buy it. I've been following this woman for half an hour. The bag sits on her body just right. The flow is pure poetry. Finally, she stopped, and is sitting right over there. It opens and closes with ease. I know because I just watched her take out her lipstick. I could see all these adorable inner pockets. I have to have that purse. All I have to do is go over there and ask her where she bought it. What if she doesn't know? Maybe it was a gift. Then, I have to convince her to give me hers. Simple. Excuse me, Miss?

# HEAD COLD

Female
Comedic
2 minutes    By Joyce Storey

Hey Mister, I'm all for family, but do you have to call your country at 3 a.m.? This alleyway between our apartments is an echo chamber and I'm trying to get some sleep here. Technically, I don't think I'm eavesdropping, but I can hear your whole conversation and I just can't take the noise right now. It's this cold. My head feels like it's going to explode, and I'm considering yanking my teeth out with pliers. I have to stuff tissues up my runny nostrils to get any sleep. No wonder I can't get a man in my bed; I look like a walrus. I took Theraflu two nights ago. You know, the one you mix with hot water and it feels like Mom's homemade soup? But it made me so stoned I couldn't even dream, except to dream I was stoned and then I woke up stoned and exhausted, but that didn't stop my damn teeth from aching. So, tonight I broke out the Sudafed, which kind of worked long enough to trick me into thinking I was getting better. But by bedtime I was contemplating punching myself in the jaw in hopes of knocking out a couple of teeth. And Sudafed causes "mild stimulation," which is code for, "Guaranteed to make you toss and turn for many restless hours." But I did manage a few cat naps until *you* got on the phone. Why are you looking at me that way? Oh, I forgot, I'm still wearing my walrus nostrils! You probably think you immigrated to Mars or something! It's probably a good thing you don't understand English. I'm too tired now to get into it. I wonder if I could get the *March of the Penguins* guys to do a documentary about me?

# HIKING EPIPHANY

Male/Female
Dramatic
2 minutes    By Talia Pura

Don't you love it out here? Doesn't it make you feel like anything is possible? When I was a kid, taking hikes with my dad was the best thing in the world. I've been so busy in the last few years, I'd forgotten how great it is to be out in nature. Every little problem just fades away. Just listen to the wind in the trees. The birds. Come on, let's keep going, there has to be a stream around here somewhere. I need to hear water. What do you mean, you're tired? How is that possible, we've been walking for what, a couple of hours? Okay, maybe three or four. I thought you were having fun, too. I told you to wear proper shoes. It's no wonder your feet hurt. Yes, just take a break. Sit on that log over there. Catch your breath. You do realize that this is a one-way trail, right? It isn't a loop. We are not magically going to end up where we started any minute now. Is that what you thought? Well, what do you want me to do? I can't carry you. We've got to go back the way we came to get to the car. Jeez, you seemed really keen on this when we started out. I had no idea you thought we'd only be out here for a few minutes. Have you never hiked before? Really, not ever? How is that possible? How have I known you this long without knowing that? Okay, it's all right. No, I'm not mad, but you are going to have to stand up and walk out of here on your own two feet.

# HITTING BOTTOM

Male
Dramatic
2 minutes   By Joyce Storey

My name is Paul. Two weeks ago, I lost my job. I come from Pennsylvania. People said yeah, come out here. Get a job, take responsibility and help your parents. I lost my job and I can't take that responsibility. Ladies and gentlemen, please help me out with a cup of coffee. I'd like to get something to eat but a cup of coffee or a butter roll will do. It's not easy standing up in front of all you people — while you pretend you're not listening. But I know you are. Judging me with your little mental score card. I see you looking out of the corner of your eye; I see it. I know you're sizing me up. Don't deny it. You look down on people like me, don't you? Think you're better than me? Is that it? Well, guess what? You probably are. But I don't give a shit. All I want is enough money to make it back home to my family. I tried out your big city and it stinks. I'm worse off than I was when I got here. I haven't seen a square meal for three days. And three square meals? Forget about it. I'll tell you why they call it, "The city that never sleeps." It's because you can't sleep in a cardboard box. Or God forbid, you don't even have a box. The concrete is hard and cold and filthy. So, if you donate to my cause just a little and someone else does and someone else does, I promise you this: I will get out of town and never look back. Because this hellhole ain't for me.

# I AM TAMIKA

Female
Dramatic
2 minutes    By Joyce Storey

*I* am Tamika. How dare you violate my name? You've smeared my *reputation*! How can we even be blood? You with your rap sheet and me with a degree from Stanford? Your mother started this. My mother told her she would name me Tamika and two weeks before I came into the world, you pop out and she gave *you my name*! Without an ounce of remorse. Who does that? You were tainted from the day you were christened. No wonder you're no good. Phony checks, phone scams, drugs. I've spent my whole life answering for *your* crap. You're like having some evil alter ego. You've ruined my whole life! One stupid clerk mixes up our social security numbers and suddenly I'm a felon! And my credit is shit! Even my Venmo is frozen! I bet I've wasted a quarter of my life trying to prove my identity to the IRS. You're a blight from birth that won't go away. And you know what makes it worse? It's *legal* for you to walk around saying you're me. Well, you're not me. And you never will be. Ever. But here I am bailing your ass out of jail. You're getting a free ride because I can't have another stain on my reputation. *Mine*. You have dragged me through the mud long enough. I have filed the papers for you to change your name. Oh, it wasn't hard. I'm *you* now, according to the universe, so if I'm going to clean up your mess, you're going to defecate on someone else's name. From now on you're Shaniqua Johnson — just like your sorry-ass mother. You can drag her name down to hell with you for all I care. Just stay away from mine.

# I HATE IKEA!

Male/Female
Comedic
2 minutes   By Talia Pura

I don't get this. I really don't. The instructions don't make any sense. I'm not a stupid person, and these instructions are written in English, but they may as well not be. Let me say this just once more, okay? I HATE IKEA! I hate it, I hate it! I don't care if we saved money. I would rather go into debt for the rest of my life than buy something I have to put together myself. Why should I have to build my own furniture? Yes, I know you are helping. Thank you. It's a big help. I'm sorry, but I think sarcasm is exactly what is called for at a time like this. I can't believe I let you talk me into this. I don't know why you find their stuff so irresistible. It's not that great. When we finally get this piece of shit built, I'm not even going to like it. At the rate we're going, it will probably fall apart the first time we sleep on it — which will not be tonight, I have to tell you. I'm exhausted and do not plan to stay awake long enough to get this ugly bed put together. No, I didn't say it was ugly in the store because you clearly loved it and I didn't want to disappoint you. Now, I no longer care. Oh, hey, hey, I'm sorry. I'm just upset, okay? Look, I didn't mean it. Honestly, I love this bed. I do, and it's going to look great. I was just frustrated, that's all. Now, tell you what. Let's just go to bed, in our old bed, just this once more. I'll call my dad in the morning and let him put it together. He loves this shit. He'll be thrilled.

# I HATE MY SISTER!

Female
Comedic
2 minutes    By Joyce Storey

I hate my sister! She has some nerve going into my closet and wearing that dress — tonight of all nights! Oh, no. Don't go defending her like you always do. You were the one who insisted she be our third roommate. But you don't know her like I do. She knew I was planning to wear it. I have my hot date with Jamal and she takes off with my dress — and where are my heels? Oh no, she didn't! Crap! She did! Those were mine! I've been paying them off for months! Now what am I gonna wear? She did this on purpose! She always was jealous of me! Oh yes, she was! When we were growing up. I'd have someone over and she'd always be right there in the middle demanding attention. And once I went out with this guy and we came home late and our parents were away and she came at me with double barrels: She didn't know where I was, something could've happened, how dare I take advantage when she was in charge? And then she busted me for lifting her ID out of her purse! I was gonna give it back. It was high school for gawd's sake. Everyone used fake IDs. Just because she never had a life didn't mean I couldn't. And now here we go again. I got this one big night out just for me and Jamal and here she goes raining on my parade. A-gain! And where's she going anyway that she needs to look all cute? It's not like she has a boyfriend. What? Everything's in the bathroom? She steamed it out for me? Wanted my night to be perfect? Aw, that's sweet! Oh, now I really hate her! She's being all nice and considerate and I look like a jerk!

# I'LL DO RIGHT BY YA

Male
Dramatic
2 minutes    By Joyce Storey

I might not be book smart but I can fix just about anythin' ya can think of. Cars, boats, tractors, fridgerators. I grew up takin' things apart in my daddy's shed. I'd lay all the parts out just right so's I knew what's what. That's the secret. Sometimes Daddy'd even scratch his head 'bout things but we'd figger it out together. He figgered two heads was better 'en one. It meant the world when he said I did good. Ya ever have that with yer daddy? Or was yours a mean son of a gun? My friend Chuck, his daddy was as mean as they come. Good thing Chuck was fast. He could outrun anybody. I wonder if most school track stars is runnin' from somethin' like Chuck was. I mean, why do they run around in a circle just to end up where they started? I been runnin' in my own circle tryin' ta get a job. Everyone wants ya ta have a degree for everythin' but it don't take no degree to take things apart. I'm real good with these new cars with the computers in 'em, too. I just take 'em apart, study 'em and buy the parts on the internet. I taught myself the internet. It wasn't hard, really. I took my whole computer apart first. Wanted ta know what I was dealin' with so I could figger out how ta use it. (*Pause*) Ta tell ya the truth, I'm kinda desperate. I got a little baby at home and a new wife and I really wanna look after 'em right, like Daddy did for me. I just need a chance, ya know? Didn't you ever need that? Please, Mister. I'm honest and hard workin' and I'll do right by ya. I promise.

# IT'S A SIGN!

Male/Female
Comedic
2 minutes    By Joyce Storey

I love signs! People write the craziest stuff on them.
Sometimes they're funny on purpose. You know, clever.
Like the sign on the funeral home that says, "Drive
carefully — we'll wait." And sometimes they leave
room for interpretation like, "Slow Children Crossing."
You usually see it in school zones or in the burbs. Now,
what I wanna know is where are all the fast kids?
Did they speed across the street so quickly they don't
warrant a sign? Maybe they're like the Roadrunner
and all you see is a cloud of dust behind them. And are
the slow children impossibly slow like decrepit old
folks or just marginally slow? Or does the sign refer
to their IQ? Did they have to take some sort of SAT-
type exam to find out if they are, in fact, slow? Is that
legal? Or ethical? Did it give them a complex when
they found out they were "slow"? Or did anyone give
them the courtesy of telling them they are in the "slow"
category? And does that apply to kids who are just
slow in math? Or do they discriminate against certain
subjects? Isn't the label of being "slow" discriminatory
in and of itself? But back to school subjects, if you're
slow at grammar is that okay cuz most people *are*
these days, so you don't need a sign? Or does it mean
the poor kids have to have an injury to count as "slow
children"? You have to have a sprained ankle or better
to constitute crossing in front of the sign. And that's

another question: Do they cross in front of the sign or can they cross behind it? And who lets them know? And what if they're not old enough or smart enough to read the damn sign in the first place? You know, come to think of it, signs can be a lot of hassle.

# JUMPING SHIP

Male/Female
Dramatic
2 minutes    By Joyce Storey

Tugboats should be called push boats. I never see them tug anything. They just push everything around. I mean, it's amazing watching them push those big barges. Little tugs against the world! Just kickin' ass and takin' names. That's who I wanna be. A badass. I think I can pull it off. I mean, right now I'm scared to death half the time. No one talks about life after college. You're just so busy getting good grades and beating your classmates and trying to please everybody from your professors to your parents that you don't think about what's going to happen afterward. But here I am. Shit. I mean, I've got this job but it really sucks and I don't think I'm a desk person, you know? What happened to conquering the world? I don't want to be some stiff suit sitting in the lunchroom talking about how much money I'm going to make when I retire. Holy crap. Is this really what life has come down to? Look at those little tugboats that don't really tug anything. They don't have a care in the world. Nobody told them they were David and the barges were Goliath. Screw this crap. I quit. I mean, if I don't quit, I'm going to turn into these flat-footed people with their heads bowed and their spirits broken. No way. That's not for me. I want to be a push boat who doesn't even mind being misnamed. I'm going to push my way to the top. But not this top. Maybe Mount Everest or something meaningful. I don't think the rat race will miss this rat. I haven't been here long enough to become a rat, I hope, so I'm jumping ship right now! I'm gonna be a tugboat or bust!

# LET IT GO

Male/Female
Comedic
2 minutes    By Joyce Storey

You say let it go like that's easy but I don't know how. I should have handled it better. I just blew up at the poor guy like it was his fault the stupid company signed me up for a recurring order. He's probably some actor who hates his job but has to do it to make rent. And he works for this crappy company because he has a flexible schedule that allows him to audition. But if I don't yell at him, who am I supposed to yell at? It's so sketchy. You buy their product while you're mindlessly playing your game on your app that's full of pop-ups and this thing looks interesting at 11 o'clock at night. But it's really crap and you tell yourself you'll never order from one of those crappy ads again. And it cost you 60 bucks but lesson learned and you forget about it and keep playing your dumb game. But then you get a package in the mail a month later with a bill for 155 bucks! That's a lot of money! And you call the guy and he tells you it's company policy and you can't get a refund. Are you kidding me? That's like a bait-and-switch or something, isn't it? It makes me so mad that they do that! It was probably buried in the fine print somewhere, but who can read all the legal crap they write these days? So here I am strapped with more expensive crap that I don't want because the first crap was crap in the first place! Now I'm all worked up again! Don't you DARE tell me to let it go! It's not right! I'm calling that actor guy back and I'm gonna unload on him AGAIN because I'm frustrated and I don't know what else to do!

# LETTER FIASCO

Male/Female
Comedic
2 minutes   By Talia Pura

There, I did it. I mailed that sucker. I pushed it through the slot and it is gone. I didn't want to give myself time to second-guess it. Why shouldn't someone hear what you really think about them? And what better way to do it than by a good old-fashioned letter? Writing it all out by hand gives you a chance to carefully craft your thoughts into the perfect prose. He should appreciate the care that went into me telling him off. I don't care if he hates me for it and never wants to speak to me again. I wonder if anything I wrote could actually be considered libelous? Is there anything in that letter that he could actually take to court? Naw, he wouldn't. Or would he? Maybe I went too far. I accused him of things I can't actually prove. Whatever, they might as well be true. Maybe I shouldn't have said that I've talked about him to a lot of other people who could hurt his career. Maybe I shouldn't have threatened him. Oh God, this was a bad idea. It felt good to write it, but I should never have sent it. If only I hadn't mailed it. I can't get it back. My hand won't fit in the slot. What if I wait until the truck comes to get it? I could ask for it back. That's reasonable. I'm the one who wrote it. I wonder how often they do a pickup? Will I have to camp out here? Wait — I was in such a hurry to mail it that I forgot the stamp. Oh, thank God. It won't go through without a stamp! I'm saved! From now on, I'll stick to emails. They're easier to delete!

# LIFE COACH

Male/Female
Comedic
2 minutes    By Talia Pura

It's okay. Not to worry. Chin up. It's just one mile at a time. Life, is just one mile at a time. I know you hate cheap philosophy, but it seems appropriate right now. The sky is always darkest before the dawn. To every cloud, there is a silver lining. For every bleak moment, there is a sunbeam waiting to find you. Well, you get the idea. I know everything seems horrible right now, but if you give yourself time, you'll feel better. I know it doesn't seem like it now, but you are going to be so happy, so very, very soon. Why not? You've got everything going for you. You've got your whole, entire life ahead of you. You just have to make it through today, and tomorrow will be better. You've got your health, right? Well, besides that hacking cough that sounds like it's turning in pneumonia, but I'm sure it won't last. You're young — you'll fight it off. Only old people die from pneumonia. Okay, so, like your emotional health, your physical health is bound to improve very soon. What else? You got a raise last week, right? That feels good, doesn't it? It does suck that your rent increase is more than your raise — but not by that much, right? And you have undeniably great hair. That counts for a lot. So much. I would kill for hair like yours. You have better hair than anyone else I know. So, there you go. How can you possibly stay depressed with hair like yours, huh? Come on, let's see a smile, okay? Just a little one. Turn that frown upside down. There you go! Wow, I'm good at this, right? I knew I could help you feel better. I should do this for a living. I'd be a great life coach!

# LOSER BOYFRIEND

Female
Dramatic
2 minutes   By Talia Pura

I'm so glad that you agreed to meet with me. I didn't know where else to turn. I mean, I tried talking to my friend, Marcy, but she was no help at all. She never liked Brad anyway. It doesn't help to simply be told, "He's a jerk, throw him out." It's more complicated than that. Isn't it? I mean, yes, of course, he is a jerk, anyone can see that. But I have invested my life into this relationship. We've been together for a long time. I can't even imagine not being with him. I love him. And he counts on me. He needs me. How could he possible manage without me? Yes, I know he's a slob who doesn't pick up after himself, and doesn't help cook or clean. He plays video games when I'd rather go out somewhere — see friends, go to a movie, anything! Anything is better than sitting at home watching someone else play video games. (*beat*) What are his good qualities? Hmm, well, ah, he — he once told me I was pretty. Several times, actually, as recently as last month, he told me I was pretty. Well, he didn't actually say pretty, but when I was dressing for that award ceremony, and asked what he thought when I was done, he did say I looked fine. I wanted him to go with me, but he wasn't interested. Not his thing, you know? Getting dressed up and going out — to a boring awards ceremony — where I was being honored. Oh, God, huge red flag, right? Totally jerk behavior. Why is it so difficult to walk away from a jerk? Yes, he's a jerk, but he's my jerk, you know? I really, really need your help here.

# LOVE IN THE FAST LANE

Male
Comedic
2 minutes   By Joyce Storey

I hate driving in midtown. The lanes are small, the traffic's bad — but hey, that girl's really cute. I mean really cute! Looks like she's been on quite the shopping spree. Prada, Gucci, Steve Madden. She must really like shoes or something. Should I stop and offer her a ride? Or is that creepy? Should I shout out and ask for her Instagram? If I don't say anything, she's never gonna know I exist and that would just be wrong. I'm the guy she's been dreaming of right here just a few feet away and she doesn't even know it! Wow, she's really hot. I mean off the charts hot! She's the perfect one for me. I wish I'd borrowed Dad's car today. It's a chick magnet. She'd sure notice me in that. Why is it that old guys are the ones who can afford the best cars? I mean, my dad doesn't need all that mojo. It's just wasted on him. Me, on the other hand, what that coupe could do for me at this second. I would have a hot babe sitting in the passenger seat, her hair flowing in the breeze. I'd crank up my playlist and the world would be perfect. Oh no, the traffic's letting up. Oh, this is bad. No, no, stop! Can't you do more construction or something? This is not the time to be speeding up. And she's rounding a corner! This is all going bad really fast! I'm speeding up and she's turning a corner. I'm doomed for life! I might as well give up now. She was going to be the woman behind the man and I'd be great and I'd be the man behind her and she'd be great. And all those kids and grandkids that will never be born! Oh, my day is ruined. Why didn't I take the bypass so I wouldn't know what I missed?

# LOVE ME OR DON'T

Male/Female
Dramatic
1 minute   By Joyce Storey

Okay, I messed up! I swear it won't happen again. Just please don't be mad at me. It kills me when you're mad. The last time we had a fight I didn't sleep for two days. Can't we talk about this like normal people and skip over that passive-aggressive stuff where you don't talk to me but make it perfectly clear I'm in the doghouse? Oh, now I've offended you twice! Great! You'll probably double down and I won't sleep for *four* days. You act all high and mighty like you're above reproach and I'm supposed to throw myself at your feet like I'm the worst person who ever walked the earth — and beg for mercy for every lousy thing I've ever done. You always dredge up the past and rehash a whole bunch of junk since the beginning of us. Well, I've had enough of all that crap. Either you love me or you don't but I'm not going to be treated like some inferior human being and suck up to you for 48 hours every time I screw up. I'm not. I'm just not.

# MAN IN THE MOON

Male/Female
Comedic
2 minutes    By Joyce Storey

Did the Man in the Moon get glasses? He looks like he's wearing glasses, doesn't he? The more I stare at him, the more he looks like he's making faces at me. Do you think he looks kind of pissed off? Maybe he's having a bad day? Or night, I guess, technically? Do you think it's night on the moon all the time? That would be a royal drag. Who wants to live in the dark all the time? But then the dude seems to glow a lot so I guess it's never really dark. It must be tough being alone up there with no arms or legs. You don't get to walk around and stretch or do anything. You just stare down at all these people who are on chillax mode because the day is over and they're kicking back with a beer listening to music or watching Netflix. Maybe that's why he got the glasses. He can't see what's on the screen. All that blue light is bad for the eyes. Especially when a lot of people watch things on small screens now — their iPhones and whatnot. And forget about Apple Watches. He probably can't read those from way up there. He's better off watching people's big-ass screens. You know, like those guys watching the football game jumping around yelling when the wrong team scores. No wonder the Man in the Moon has bifocals. There must be so much to watch that his head is on a swivel. Maybe that's why he goes down to a crescent every now and again just to get some rest. He looks all peaceful up there just hanging out but he must be overwhelmingly stressed with everything that goes on here. No wonder he has a sourpuss look on his face. I think he needs a good shrink.

# MARRIAGE FREAK-OUT

Male
Dramatic/Comedic
2 minutes   By Talia Pura

Married! She wants to get married. Now. What year does she think this is? 1955? She wants to get married and start making babies! I'm far too young to get married. I know that my mother had me when she was younger than I am now, but she got pregnant and thought she had to follow through. Well, don't get me wrong, I'm happy to be here, but we have options now. I may never be ready to get married and have kids. I can't raise a kid. I have no parenting skills whatsoever. I can't even imagine it. I have a hard time deciding what to have for lunch, never mind choosing to settle down with one person for the rest of my life. I love my girlfriend. I do, sort of. I like hanging out with her, most of the time, but marrying her? I don't think so. I don't know. How can I possibly know? Waking up to her every day for the rest of my life? Well, probably not the rest of my life — divorce rates being what they are. And hey, if I'm thinking that now, she is clearly not the one. She kind of freaked out at my reaction. How could she think I'd be thrilled? Why did she feel the need to propose? Why couldn't we just let things unfold naturally? Why did she have to push it? She took a perfectly functioning relationship, and flat-out ruined it. Now it's just weird. What am I supposed to do? Call her and apologize for freaking out? How does that end? With me saying yes to her proposal? That can't happen. So, great, just great. I guess it ends. The relationship, I mean. It's over. There's nowhere to go from here. Wow, well, I guess I'm single again.

# MEET THE PARENTS

Female
Dramatic
2 minutes    By Talia Pura

Yes, this one is perfect. I wore it to my parents' twenty-fifth anniversary party. It's parent tested. And he said his family dresses for dinner. Do I want to belong to a family that dresses for dinner? I can't do this. I don't want to meet his parents. Not yet. Of course, they will wonder why I backed out. I have to go. I am good enough for their son. He loves me and it doesn't matter what they think. Okay, it does matter. I will live to regret it if his parents don't like me. Wear anything, he said. You always look great. They'll like me. Why wouldn't they? Because they will take one look at me and decide that I look like a flower. It's too fussy, too flouncy, too much! This dress is much better. No frills, no fuss. But, maybe the neckline is too low, and it's too short. I'll look like a hooker. Their son picked me up on a street corner. I need something that says I'm my own person, confident, independent. Someone who doesn't care that their son has money, or loves him for his money. This skirt is perfect. It says all of those things. It also says Gypsy. They'll think I'm there to read their cards. A suit. You can never go wrong with a simple, tasteful suit. Nice clean lines, dark, unpretentious. And business. Like I'm there to analyze stock portfolios. I have nothing to wear!  Nothing! I know! I'll wear what I wore for our first date. It's perfect. He'll think it's sweet that I'm wearing it again. He said he fell in love with me on our first date. Why wouldn't his parents, too?

# MINIMUM WAGE

Female
Dramatic
2 minutes    By Joyce Storey

What's *not* on my resume? You really want to know? I make $11.00 an hour and I'm one paycheck away from despair. After bills, I've got $30 a month to buy food. My daughter doesn't deserve to live this way. Look at her picture. Isn't she beautiful? I almost called Child Services to come and take her, but she wouldn't let me. I broke my wrist last year. I couldn't work and had no health care, so I lost my apartment and moved into my car with my daughter. What kind of mother does that to her child? I'm so ashamed. A shelter? I finally got us into one. It's humiliating and dangerous. My daughter isn't allowed to be there unsupervised and I don't get home until 7:30 p.m. because I sold the car to buy food. Now I take the bus an hour and a half each way. She's out of school at 3 o'clock. My 13-year-old baby has to roam the streets for four and a half hours until I come home to be with her at the shelter. I pray every day that God will keep her safe until I get there. When I think of what could happen... I'm trying, I really am. I found a cheap apartment, but I don't make enough to cover the rent. I'm all she's got and I'll be damned if I'm going to let her down. So, now you know. I called in sick today to meet you. If my boss finds out, she'll fire me. If you hire me and give me a good wage, I'll work harder than anyone you've ever met. But if you don't, I hope you see her picture in your mind every night when you go to sleep, because now her welfare is in your hands.

# MISERABLE AIRPORTS

Male
Comedic
2 minutes   By Joyce Storey

Airports piss me off! Look around you. Miserable people everywhere trying to make other people miserable. Even if you start your day in a good mood, by the time you've spent an hour in the airport, you're done. You employees are miserable because you spend your entire day dealing with miserable asshole travelers. And at the end of the day, the miserable asshole is less than miserable — sipping Mai Tais on some beach in Mozambique, while the poor sucker ticketing agent goes home miserable to get ready for his next miserable day of work. Meanwhile, I get up at 5:30 in the morning to catch my flight because the only one that wasn't booked leaves at some ungodly hour of the morning. I get here and the place is a zoo. Did all these people really get their asses out of bed as early as me? Apparently so. I check in by machine because the ticketing line is from here to Honolulu and really, who wants to deal with people before the coffee kicks in, anyway? Ultimately, I gotta get on the miserable line with the miserable people and the miserable security agent. No belt, no shoes, no coats, no respect. One freakazoid ignites his sneakers and I'm dodging athlete's foot for years to come. I had a connecting flight in 10 minutes. Was it my fault my incoming plane was late? Of course not. Did the miserable asshole working the line expedite me? You know he didn't.

That's $1,300 bucks down the miserable drain. WTF? Ever see an airline commercial with miserable people? Hell, no! They're all warm and fuzzy. Well, I for one, demand you start hiring warm and fuzzy people and fire all the miserable jerks. Have a nice freaking day, you miserable asshole!

# MORE THAN SUGAR

Female
Dramatic
2 minutes   By Joyce Storey

Ray-Ray boy you got some nerve coming over here lookin' like that. All sweet and sugar and lookin' fine. What you doing? You think I'm falling for this stuff. "Oh, DeWanda, you lookin' good. You the only one for me." Yeah, yeah I know all about it Ray-Ray. You're all sweet on me for about 10 minutes until your head goes on a swivel when you walk down the street and you see all those hot young things. It's a wonder you head don't fall off, it turns so fast. We've been down this road before, you and me. Too many times. Way too many times. I'm tired of pickin' up your underwear and tossin' it in the laundry and cookin' you a good breakfast and sendin' you off to who knows where you go all day. It ain't work, I know that much. You don't bring nothing home and we got two little kids right in there in that other room and they is sound asleep and they got to be fed and they got to be clothed and they got to be loved. Now I know you love them. I really do. But you don't got the first clue how to look after those two beautiful little angels. They always asking: "Where's daddy? When he gonna come take us to the zoo like you promised? When he gonna come give us a ride in that new car he talking about? When he gonna show up?" So now you showed up. And they sleepin' and I ain't wakin' 'em up. No, sir. It takes more than sugar and sweet smelling cologne, Ray-Ray. It takes hard work and commitment. You even know what commitment means? Look it up online and when you figure out what that means — what it really means — you come callin' again. But until then, don't come sniffing around here. I got better things to do.

# MY NAME IS CAROLINE

Female
Dramatic
2 minutes   By Joyce Storey

My name is Caroline. Car-oh-line. Like fishing line or clothesline. I live my life in a straight line. Straight to high school, straight to college, straight to my first job. Straight to hell in a handcart. Nobody told me doing everything right would be so stressful and boring and soooo unimaginative. I did what my parents expected and all my aunts and uncles and cousins told me I was great and now look at me. I graduated *summa cum laude* and I'm in an accounting pool. Accounting! Could I get more boring and predictable? How did I turn into a nobody? And so fast? Is this what life is? Sitting at a desk 'til my butt gets flat? When does it get fun? I didn't take a gap year like Matty and go hiking in the Himalayas or volunteer with Doctors Without Borders. I was too busy being perfect. And where did that get me? Someday, I can aspire to getting my own office and maybe it'll have a window. I'll work late and eat cold pizza and get pudgy because I didn't start my day at the gym and I'm too tired when I get home from work. Gaaaaawd! I have my whole dull life mapped out and I don't even have time for kids! So here you go. My resignation. I'm going to Peru to see Machu Picchu and maybe I'll have an epiphany about how to earn money when I get back. Or maybe I won't. But I will die here before my twenty-fifth (*change according to appropriate age*) birthday if I stay. Who knew a straight line could be so soul crushing? I think I'll start spelling my name "Carolyn" with an l-y-n just to shake things up. I need to DO something with my life. Because I only get one and, so far, I'm wasting it.

# NEAR MISS

Male/Female
Dramatic
1 minute   By Talia Pura

Oh my God, did you see that? That guy nearly creamed me! That was so close! What the hell was he thinking? He must have been on his cell or something. It's called hands on the wheel, eyes on the road, buddy! I'm driving a bright red car, you moron, don't tell me you didn't see me! Why does no one in this city drive well? Everyone bought cars with optional turn signals? Speed limits are just a suggestion? And traffic lights? A red light doesn't actually mean you have to stop, does it? I have never had to be such a defensive driver in my life. That was the second accident I've avoided this week alone. Is it any wonder you see crosses and memorials at every other street corner? People in this city can't drive worth a damn. I think I have to move before I become a statistic.

# NEW COUNTRY

Male/Female
Dramatic
2 minutes   By Joyce Storey

You wouldn't understand. How could you? This is a new country for me. You don't get what that means. Different food, different customs. Different everything. I've never lived in a city and I have to figure out public transit in a new language. I've been late for class three times because I took the wrong bus. I'm barely able to follow a conversation with you and your friends. You use all these words that aren't in Google Translate so I'm totally lost. I just kind of laugh and nod and pretend I know what's going on but I don't have a clue. And then I'm supposed to take classes and keep up and everything. But I barely understand what the professor is saying and if I don't get good grades, my parents will disown me. They gave up everything to move us here. Everything. Career, money, friends, family. And now my father's a taxi driver and my mother can't get a job because she doesn't speak English. They want a better life for my brother and me so they have sacrificed theirs. If I don't get As in everything, I mean everything, right across the board, what is their sacrifice for? They want me to come home and do my family chores and study hard and live up to their expectations. That's my part of the bargain. There's so much pressure on me; I feel like I'm going to explode. I can barely read the piles of assignments I have. Forget about actually doing them. And what do I know about science anyway? And anatomy? I faint at the sight of blood. How am I going to be a doctor if I can't even pass introductory biology? So no, I can't go to the bar with you and "hang out." I feel like I want to hang myself.

# OUTDOOR TYPE

Male/Female
Dramatic
2 minutes   By Talia Pura

No, it's fine — you go ahead. Find out if that water is drinkable. I'll just wait here. (*alone now*) Really, just leave me here to die in peace. No, I don't actually mean that. I love my life, and I need you to find my way out of here. I thought that we were going to take a walk in a nice civilized park on a trail marked with little stick men carrying backpacks, and then go out to a restaurant for dinner. Why did I lie about being a huge "lover of the great outdoors"? I like my environment clean and sanitized. I'm sorry I misled you. I could really use a cigarette. Why, oh why, did I present myself as a non-smoker? I'm going to pass out from all this fresh air. He can't really be thinking that this is fun! I should find him down at that watering hole and admit everything. He won't even want to see me again if he knows that I smoke and I hate hiking. What do we even have in common? Aside from our taste in restaurants... and movies, and views on politics and religion. We laugh at the same jokes. He makes me feel good about myself. Like I can do anything! But that's not good. That's what got me on this hideous hike in the first place. I actually thought I could do it! Well, maybe that's not such a bad thing. It is beautiful out here. If I stopped smoking, those hills would be easy to climb. There are worse things than being outside in great weather. I could stand it once in a while. I should get out more, enjoy the great outdoors, fill my lungs with fresh air. (*big breath, little cough*) Nothing like a little walk in the woods on a sunny day. (*calls out*) Hey, James, how's the water?

# OVER

Female
Dramatic
2 minutes   By Joyce Storey

Who's he kidding? He always says I can get anybody. Like he's daring me to cheat, ya know? I never say that cuz that's not where my head is at. That's not where my heart is. But he keeps pushing and pushing, so I tell him I been stepping out for years, just like he says. Got me a real man, someone who's not jealous, in his own bones. Let's me be who I am. Loves me and all that crap. And it *is* crap. I never even looked at another guy. I just wanted *him*. But today, I don't know, I just snapped. I was all sarcastic and I thought he knew it, but it only made him mad. And the madder he got, the madder I got. Just kinda spiraled out of control. I don't know what happened, but it's over. So, let him move on. I totally get it. I do. I guess. ...Okay, I lied. I totally don't get anything. He's gone and I'm scared. And mad and hurt. I gave him everything. Everything! But he had to keep picking at us all the time. How long before he'll file for divorce? Hopefully, soon. You gotta tell him I wanna get this over with. What's wrong with that dumbass, anyway? I just wanted him to want me. That's all I ever asked. If that's too much, what does that make me? Unlovable? Am I really that hideous? How dare he? He walks all over me and then walks out on me. Well, good riddance. I'm tired of trying to build him up. I gotta work on myself. I gotta get back out there. I gotta... I'm sorry. I gotta cry. Just cry. Nobody may ever want me again. I never thought this would ever happen to me. If love's not enough, what is?

# PACKAGING NIGHTMARE

Male/Female
Comedic
1.5 minutes   By Talia Pura

What is the point of this wrapping? Why does a potato chip bag have to be impenetrable? Sure, you want it to be fresh and all. No one wants stale or soggy chips. But this is ridiculous! I've been at it for half an hour. I cannot break in. Now everyone is looking at me. Do you know how lame it is to not be able to break the seal on a bag of chips? I spent ten minutes looking for a tiny break in the surface indicating a tearaway. Nothing. Another ten, at least, grabbing each side and trying to pull it apart. No luck. If I'd thought to bring a pair of scissors… Yeah, right! Doesn't everyone riding the subway carry scissors? It would probably be considered a weapon. This isn't a case of strength or ingenuity. Without a tool there is no way of gaining entry. I'm tempted to put it on the floor and stomp on it. See if it won't break open then! Problem is, the chips would be smashed and fly all over the car. I'd probably be fined for littering. So, I have two choices: Take this bag home and cut it open, or leave it here for some poor slob to find and think they've been treated to a free bag of chips. Yeah, I think that's the way to go. I no longer want anything to do with this bag of chips, and will never buy this brand again. *Adios*, demon spawn from the chip factory! Time to mess with someone else's day.

# PARENTS

Male/Female
Dramatic
2 minutes    By Talia Pura

I can't believe I have to say this again! I've told you over and over that I can't be caught in the middle. Oh, God! You guys are adults! I spent my entire childhood either getting out of your way or trying to be the referee. Do you know how relieved I was when you finally split up? I know, I know, you stayed together for my sake. You meant well, I understand that, but it was a stupid idea. Neither of you could stand the other. I don't know what brought you together in the first place! Okay, yes, I remember you told me you thought he was cute. Cute is not a good reason to marry someone. And then, just when you knew you should leave, you got pregnant, and you wanted me to have a dad. Great, that's great. And he is a pretty good dad, he really is, but he was an even better dad when he didn't have to live with you anymore. I'm sorry, I know that hurts a bit, but it's the truth. It wasn't all him, you know. It wasn't a simple case of marrying a jerk. He is not a jerk, and no, I'm not saying it was all your fault, either. You are both decent people who have nothing in common and no reason to be together. I can manage just fine on my own, and see each of you whenever you like. I don't need to see you both at the same time. I never want a repeat of my high school graduation party. That was painful. If I ever get married, I guess I'll have to have two weddings, one for each of you. Unless you can both manage to grow up enough to remain civil, and each stay on your own side of the room.

# PARTY CENTRAL

Male/Female
Comedic
2 minutes    By Joyce Storey

If this is gonna be party central, it has to have a wet bar.
This isn't some college frat party where you throw a
kegger and everyone drinks 'til they pass out. This is
the real world now. We need to step up our game and
be responsible adults. We're announcing to the world
that we are here! I got us business cards and everything.
Vistaprint rocks! Look, they're kinda psychedelic. They
sent enough to paper the wall. What do you say? Should
we do it? It might be a cool statement. Or maybe we
could get one of those vinyl posters with our faces on
it and hang it from the balcony so people see it when
they walk into the building. And we could have another
one cut into puzzle pieces so they have an activity to do.
We could glue up a whole wall and they could stick the
puzzle pieces on it. But then if they make a mistake, it
might be hard to pry the glue off and we don't want our
faces looking disfigured if they get the pieces wrong, like
the eyeballs hanging down too low or something. Maybe
that's not such a hot idea. Do you think we should we go
with more traditional mixers like Twister and Flip Cup?
Good thing they haven't banned plastic cups yet. Flip Cup
wouldn't be right with real glasses. I got the red ones.
They hold a lot of beer. (*beat*) What? Who cares about a
business plan? That takes too much time and they'll be
so wasted they won't care. We'll just wing it and they'll be
dying to invest. I bought enough food and drinks to last
us through the apocalypse. This is gonna be awesome!
We're gonna rock the house and storm the castle!

# PERFORMING AGAIN

Male/Female
Dramatic
2 minutes   By Talia Pura

Practicing bores me beyond words! I hate practicing. I should never have promised to play this concert. Why did I think it was a good idea? Why? I spent my entire childhood playing this piano, and I hated almost every minute of it. Okay, I did actually enjoy the recitals. And, okay, yes, it's probably because I was very good at it. I won contests, lots of them. I never got nervous or anything. But I quit for a reason! A very good reason. I did not enjoy the practicing. And even if you are a bit of a prodigy, you still have to practice — a lot! So why did I think it would be fun to play this concert — just this one little concert — for old times' sake? What kind of a dumb idea was that? How did I get talked into this? Prestigious or not, I should have said no. After all, I'm not trying to build a career here. I've moved on. The piano is no longer my life. What was I thinking? I can't just pick up where I left off five years ago. It doesn't work that way. I figured it would. Like riding a bicycle. You don't have to relearn how to ride a bike after five years, right? And I was good! I was really good! And these pieces are not particularly difficult. I should be able to just rattle them off! But my fingers are not cooperating. They won't move fast enough. And now that I am committed, I can't look like an idiot out there. People will expect this to be half decent. I must practice. I have to practice. Okay fingers, let's do this, and I promise you'll never have to touch a piano again!

# PICK-UP LINE

Male
Comedic
2 minutes   By Talia Pura

Hey, pretty lady. You're looking mighty lonely, sitting over here all by yourself. You aren't meeting anyone here, are you? I mean, if you are waiting for your boyfriend or your husband or something, I'll just be on my way. But I have this feeling that you and I were meant to meet here tonight. You're too pretty a lady to spend the evening alone. I don't see a ring on your finger or nothing. I notice things like that. So, what do you say to a little "getting to know each other" drink? I won't take no for an answer. Bartender? The lady would like another — what are you drinking? A margarita? Wow, classy drink. Sure you wouldn't rather have a beer? Just kidding. Ah, I'll have the same, bartender. Make it two margaritas, or should that be margariti? You only live once, am I right? So, what brings you out on a chilly night like this? But I do love how your sweater brings out the color of your eyes. Such a lovely shade of brown. This is my lucky day, finding you here, looking all beautiful. You were just hoping someone like me would pass by, weren't you? And here I am. Ready and willing. I haven't come in here in a long time. Sorry to keep you waiting like that. If I'd known you'd be here, I wouldn't have waited so long. I'd have been here much sooner. I — ah, wait, wait, you haven't even finished your drink. We just got started. Hey, I — I don't even know your name! Damn. (*shrugs and turns away*) Hi, you're looking awfully lonely, sitting over here all by yourself.

# PLAIN MEANS PLAIN

Male/Female
Comedic
2 minutes   By Joyce Storey

Excuse me?  Excuse me. EXCUSE ME! There seems to be some confusion here.  I ordered plain. Yes. No, it's not. No, it's not. *No, it's not.* I saw them put cheese on it. I don't *have* to open it. I saw. Can you just please have them make me a plain one? Thank-you. ...No, not that one! I don't want a pre-made one. It'll have pickles on it. The last time I got pickles, and I hate pickles. They infect the taste. You can't even cover it with ketchup. Have them make a fresh one. Well, please ask them to *break* the rules. I hate pickles. You know, I don't understand why this has to be so difficult. See this receipt? It says *double burger to go, plain.* And what always happens is, I get down the street, open it up, and find pickles on it, or cheese, and not even cheese just on top. It's melted between the patties, so you can't even scrape it off. (*beat*) But, I shouldn't *have* to check it before I leave here. You should get it right in the first place. And plain means plain. Not plain with pickles or plain with cheese. Just plain old plain. Every time I ask for plain, they say, "Do you want lettuce and tomato with that?" I say no. "Cheese?" If I wanted cheese, I would have ordered a cheeseburger. If I order it plain, I want plain! Just the bun and the meat. Got it?! Plain. What? Of course, I see the receipt. Number 6. That's me. Number 9? (*Turns receipt upside down, realizing he/ she's inverted the number*) It's not mine? It's his?  (*Looks up at a VERY large man beside him/her, intimidated.*) Oh. You know what? I changed my mind. I think I'll just go get a salad.

# PROCRASTINATION SOUP

Male/Female
Comedic
1 minute   By Talia Pura

Wow, this soup smells amazing. It is going to taste so good! I make the best soup, but only under very specific conditions. There has to be a huge, looming deadline for a very important project. A report that must be written. The bigger the report, the less I want to write it, and the greater the urge to make soup. One that requires lots and lots of ingredients: vegetables that must be carefully chopped, a quick trip to the market for just the right herbs, a broth that must be tended. It turns into an all-day event. But it is so worth it. Just smell that fabulous aroma. It's almost ready. Just as soon as I have a bowl of it, I will magically feel an overwhelming desire to sit down and write. I will, I'm sure of it — just as soon as I make some biscuits to go with the soup.

# PUPPY LOVE

Male/Female
Dramatic/Comedic
2 minutes    By Talia Pura

Training a dog is quite possibly the hardest thing I've ever taken on. I thought I was ready for a dog. We had a dog when I was a kid. Granted, we got her when I was three, so I wasn't heavily involved in training her. Ginger was always well behaved. I thought all dogs were. I loved Ginger. I knew that I'd get a dog as soon as I had my own place that was dog friendly. So, I did. Yesterday. Do I look tired right now, because I am exhausted! I hardly slept a wink. Shhh, do you hear that? Oh, please god, let her stay sleeping. I think she heard you come in. I put her in her kennel. Do you know how long it took her to settle down and fall asleep? You'd think anyone that stayed up whining all night would want to sleep all day. I know I do! Yes, I know I said we'd go out tonight, but I just can't. I won't be any fun. I won't be able to keep my eyes open. And how can I leave her alone? Once she wakes up, I have to take her for a walk immediately, and then it will be puppy playtime, and then I'll have to feed her, and, honestly, it may be well into next month before I can go out again. It's going to be awful when I go back to work on Monday, leaving her crated all day. I can't possible think about going out in the evening, too. Hey, you like dogs, right? You can stay and watch me take care of her, okay? It'll be fun. I promise. And we can go out next month.

# RATS!

Male/Female
Comedic
2 minutes   By Talia Pura

Oh, excuse me, I didn't know anyone was in here. I, ah, have you seen Angela? She was in the other room with me a minute ago, but now I can't find her. Maybe she wandered in here? No, I don't think she'll just find me when she's ready. I really need to find her. Yes, I know that independence is a good thing at a certain age, but — yes, that's right, she's very young. ...Well, let's see, how to describe her? She's white, super cute. Yes, obviously, all parents think that, but she really is. She's not very big. Eyes? Pink. ...Yes, she has pink eyes. No, not pink eye shadow, pink eyes. Not at all uncommon. Most domestic rats are white with pink eyes. ...Yes, Angela is a rat, an adorable little white rat. ...Now, just, just calm down. Stop screaming, please. She can't hurt you! She's way more afraid of you than you are of her. You really don't need to pull your feet up. ...No, she's not going to crawl up your leg. That's just a myth. You might want to check your handbag, though. I see it's open. If you have any food in there, she might have crawled inside. Hey, careful, dumping it all out like that! She — okay, I see she wasn't in there. ...Yes, I'm sure. Don't you think you'd have noticed a white rat flying through the air along with all that stuff you keep in there? But that's great, 'cause she would not have enjoyed the ride.  Angela, where are you? Come here, baby. Are you in here? Okay, there aren't many places to hide in here, apart from your handbag. I'll just leave you alone now and check the rooms down the hall. Oh, if you do see her, feel free to scream again. I'll come running.

# REDHEAD SUE

Male
Comedic
2 minutes    By Joyce Storey

Redhead Sue! My gosh, how long has it been? I haven't seen you since, what? High school? It's been a long time. Look at you. You haven't changed a bit. No, really, you look as amazing as ever. What have you been doing with yourself? Are you married? Kids? College? Did I mention how great you look? Oh, listen to me running my mouth. It's just so great to see you. I've missed you. No, really. I think about you. I had so many chances and I never once ever opened my mouth. But I wanted to. I did! You must've thought I was nuts. I'd come over to say something and I couldn't get a word out. Not one. I'd just stare at you and sputter something unintelligible and turn around and walk away. And now I can't keep a word *in*. That must be confusing for you. It's likc "Truc Confessions" right here in the maternity ward. You were the one that got away. I will never forget senior prom. You were dressed in that gorgeous red taffeta gown. Stunning. The whole room glowed when you walked in. It was like the world stopped and then started spinning in slow-mo. And me, I was so tongue-tied. I wanted to ask you to dance; I did! But the words just wouldn't come. And now in a bizarre twist of fate, it appears I will be delivering your baby. Who saw that coming, right? Don't worry, I'm a good doctor. Really, I am. But I really wish I had opened my mouth back then. And now I can't seem to close it. Now that I have put both feet in, I will shut up. But you do look great. Just saying.

# REFEREE

Male/Female
Comedic
2 minutes    By Talia Pura

Yeah! I did it! I did it! I did it! I DID IT! It was amazing. It was epic! You've never seen anything like it. Twenty-two pairs of eyes are riveted on me. The moment is NOW. I spring into action.  With a single bound, that I'm pretty sure is actually airborne for at least three seconds, I reach the two archenemies in the center of the encircling horde. STOP, I yell. They don't. Slowly they circle each other, hatred smoldering in their eyes; arms outstretched, readying themselves for the attack. STAY BACK. I warn the crowd, sensing that they might get caught in the crossfire. The crowd complies — out of fear for the destruction to come? Nay, out of respect. Respect for the swift justice that they know I can deliver. Step by cautious step I advance on the demons. Just as I am about to apprehend one, he lunges at the other, knocking him to the floor. An "ahhh" arises from the gathered throng. In a world where we teach peace and understanding, why does the mob unfailingly turn out to witness such conflict and carnage? Now that one is down, the crowd is rabid with bloodlust, sensing the kill. As his standing oppressor prepares to throw himself headlong onto his prone form, he rolls to the side and shoots to his feet. Again, both face each other. Together they lunge and are locked in mortal combat. I have no choice but to close the gap between us and physically enter the fray. I lay one firm but gentle hand on each offending shoulder. Both shudder and gasp, looking up to meet my disapproving, downward gaze. BOTH OF YOU TO THE PRINCIPAL'S OFFICE. NOW!

# REVENGE

Female
Comedic
2 minutes    By Talia Pura

Oh please, who does he think he's fooling? She's been in there for, like, an hour. That is how long it takes to deliver a package? (*looks toward closed door*) We all know what kind of package you're delivering. What kind of work environment is created when you know your boss is, like, doing the delivery girl? He thinks that because he gave me a raise and my own little office, I'll keep my mouth shut. Yeah, whatever! I am so tempted to like, just call his wife, Tiffany, and spill the beans! You should have seen that delivery girl when she came out of his office last week. She totally had *that* look, you know what I mean? Her hair was all sideways on her head and her lipstick was majorly kissed off. Last year, he was way different. He actually had some class. He always took me to lunch after we did it in his office and I would never walk out without checking myself in a mirror. Then he had the nerve to dump me. Can you believe it? He is in there right now cheating on that poor little religious girl who married him in good faith. I really feel like it may be my civic duty to make an anonymous phone call and clue Tiffany in. Maybe I could provide anonymous pictures. I could totally like burst in there right now with my cell phone camera and say, like, SURPRISE! or something, and like totally catch them in the act. I could. Or, I could give him the evil eye when she comes out, and try a little blackmail. Maybe a new title and a big fat raise.

# SAVING THE WORLD

Male
Dramatic
2 minutes    By Joyce Storey

Listen to me. I'm not your guy. I don't know what kind of prophecy or vision or message you think you had, but you're wrong about me. I'm not brave. I faint at the sight of blood. When I got picked on as a kid, I ran away. I am *not* the guy who can save the world. I can barely find two socks that match in the morning and I sure as hell don't know how to pilot a plane. Or a spaceship or flying saucer or whatever that thing is. Don't cry. Please don't cry. I'd like to help you. I really would. But I'm just a guy. I build things. I work with my hands. That's all I'm good at. I don't even have a tissue to offer you. Please stop. You'll get a headache. I get these bad ones, like a vice grip latching onto my head. I see stars and everything... Yeah, blue stars. How did you know? Yeah, with orbs circling around them. Do you get them too? What? It's not a *sign*. It's a *migraine*. It's no big deal, except I usually black out after the orbs. I wake up disoriented and exhausted like I've been traveling or something. I can't believe I'm telling you this. You must think I'm a freak. *I* think I'm a freak. And then come the bizarre dreams afterward. Yeah, recurring, like I'm stuck in a loop. I meet this emperor and he tells me I'm the only hope to save the planet; that I'm getting stronger every day and when the time comes, I'll meet... Oh, crap. It's you! You're the one! You look just like he said. And you're real. So I must be...? No. *Really*? But... Oh, God. How am I supposed to save the world? I'm from Brooklyn.

# SCHIZO

Male/Female
Darkly Comedic
2 minutes    By Joyce Storey

I killed my mother today. Psych! I didn't kill her. I just imagined it in detail. Do you think that makes me unbalanced? Oh, come on, like you've never thought about it. Everyone wants to strangle their mom at least once in a lifetime, right? It's not like I *did* it or anything. But if I had, I would have lured her into the basement. Except she has a bad hip and the stairs bother her, but I'd get her down there somehow. That's where she'd be least likely to be heard by the neighbors if she screamed or anything. But she wouldn't, because I'd sneak up behind her and hit her over the head with a hammer. Not the head of the hammer, the side. The head might go through her head. A head for a head, an eye for an eye… Never mind. If that happened, it would be bloody and messy. I don't like the sight of blood and I certainly don't want to clean it up. And the idea is just to knock her unconscious, not kill her — yet. Maybe I should use a two-by-four. Anyway, she'd die in the noose. I know what you're thinking: How would I lift her up, right? Her being dead weight and all. Not totally dead, just unconscious. Well, I've got this whole elaborate pulley system worked out. I could wrap the rope around her neck when she's on the floor and then hoist her up. See, I'd be humane about it. She probably wouldn't feel a thing. She'd be dead before she regained consciousness. …What? You think I'd want to torture my own mother? You're really sick, you know that? Sick. How can you think like that? Why am *I* the one locked up, Doc? The way I see it, you're the one who's twisted.

# SEX CHANGE

Male/Female
Dramatic
2 minutes   By Talia Pura

Look, I'm sorry. I should have told you earlier. I see that now. Don't you think I tried? I was too afraid. I started to tell you a million times, but, something always held me back. It was a hard conversation to initiate. You can understand that, right? I fell in love with you so fast. We are so good together. I know you think so, too. I told myself that it didn't matter, that you loved me for who I am, right now. I'm not who I used to be. I'm not what you think you see. You teased me for playing hard to get, because you thought I was just shy. Well, I am shy, I always have been. But, of course now you know that I was also afraid. I didn't expect to end up here tonight. If I'd known, I'd have found a way to tell you, but, it was all so spontaneous. Look, I know you're surprised. Okay, yes, shocked — you are shocked, but, I hope not dismayed. You aren't actually dismayed, are you? Bottom surgery is so expensive. It will be a while before I can get it, but the top surgery worked out really well, didn't it? You can't even hardly tell, right? And my voice — I've really worked on my voice. You never even suspected, did you? So, why do my present genitalia have to be so important to you? Please, please turn around. Please look at me. All of me. It's me. It's just still me, inside. I'm sorry that the outside doesn't quite all match who I am. It will one day. Soon, really soon. Can't we be okay until then?

# SHOPPING DILEMMA

Female
Dramatic
2 minutes   By Talia Pura

So, which one is it going to be? The red one or the blue one? Sure, I know, I've already got some great dresses to wear. I don't *need* another new dress — but that has never stopped me before. Shopping is fun! Wearing something new is fun! It's a first date! Doesn't it deserve something brand new? And they cost practically nothing. I should just buy both of them. Wow, look at all these rows and rows of clothes. It's a sea of color. It's endless, and this is only one store. This is kind of insane! Why do we need all this stuff in our lives? Why is it all so enticingly inexpensive? When did clothes get to be this cheap? What is happening? I, I can't breathe. I'm drowning in all these racks of clothes! We buy all these clothes we don't need, that are made in countries that pay wages so low that we can stock up any time we feel like it. Not to mention the chemicals going into the manufacturing of the fabric! Oh, you only buy natural fabrics? Do you have any idea what the carbon footprint of 100% cotton is? This isn't sustainable. But how can it stop? Is a terrible wage in a poor country better than no wage at all? Is manufacturing all this fabric keeping some poor family alive? I don't have the answers. What can I do to make the world better? I'm just me, just one person. So, maybe I can start right now, and not buy the red *or* the blue dress. It isn't much, but I guess it's a start until I figure out something better.

# SISTERS

Female
Dramatic
2 minutes    By Talia Pura

I am so happy that I've learned to travel light. I hope to never wait at a baggage carousel again. I am so grateful to finally sink into this airline seat, cramped as it is, and just not think about anything. My family, and all its problems can stay where they are, and I don't have to think about them until, well, maybe not until my next visit, but at least until I land. You know how it can be when you visit family. Especially my sister, who will never let go of old hurts and slights. Jealousy — that's all it is. Petty jealousy. Everybody's life looks better than our own — especially when you don't see it day to day. I was so thankful to get away from them this time. Oh, we're starting our descent. Just look at those clouds down there! Like fluffy snow covering the ground. Brilliant sunshine up here. Meagan and all her pettiness seem a million miles away up here. Wow, we are going down, right through all those clouds — it feels like going down into water. I almost feel like holding my breath. We are not breaking though these clouds. They're still all around us. It's completely socked in — what a rainy day, dull and wet. Ugh, I didn't want to come home to this. But, the sun is up there. It's a brilliant sunny sky, right above those clouds. No matter how cloudy or rainy a day, the sun is always just above you. It's there, waiting for us. I guess I'm ready to call Meagan, now. She's my sister, and I need her. We'll find some way to see the sun again.

# SORRY

Male/Female
Dramatic
2 minutes    By Talia Pura

Look, I'm sorry — although I think I should be getting an apology from you. Seriously, would it kill you to say sorry once in a while? Never mind that you didn't do anything wrong this time. There are plenty of other times when you hurt my feelings, too, and you never seem to feel the need to apologize. It's two little words. Say them, and level the playing field. I'm up at least 16 to 2 on apologies. Well, some things never change, do they? Just because you're three years older than me you think you are impervious to ever needing forgiveness? Being an older sister means never having to say you're sorry? You get to say whatever pops into your head, call me an assortment of awful names, insult my taste in dates, clothes and restaurant choices, and after all that, have the privilege of taking offense if I ever stand up for myself? I'm sorry, it doesn't work that way. I know I used the words "I'm sorry," but please don't take that as another apology. I've used up my quota for the day. In fact, I take back the one I gave you earlier. I am not sorry. I just said your couch was really big for this apartment. I didn't say it was ugly, although I could have. I merely pointed out an actual true fact. Okay, okay, I'm sorry that your apartment is too small for that couch. I'm sorry you bought it anyway, and sorry your boyfriend threw his back out getting it up the stairs. I'm sorry, I'm sorry, I'm sorry. Now, can you please back up enough to allow this door to open so I can get out of here? Thank you!

# SUCKER

Male
Dramatic
1.5 minutes   By Joyce Storey

Yo, I be standin' on this corner forever. You text me and you say you was gonna be here. And I get myself outta bed and I get myself together and I take the train down here and I be waitin' here and now you text me and say you're just gettin' on your train?! You be the one who axed me to come here. Well, bitch, I'm here and you ain't, so why I be standin' on this corner? You wanna break up or you wanna stay together? Which is it today? Because I be losin' track. You be like, "I love you, baby. I need you, I can't live without you," one minute and then you be like, "Oh you are the most annoyin' piece o' crap I ever met! I don't wanna see you, I don't wanna hear from you. Lose my number." Well, now maybe it's me who should be sayin' lose my number. I am sick and tired o' bein' sick and tired o' this. You hear me? You pickin' up what I'm puttin' down? You text me and you say be here and I be here. Well, I ain't makin' that mistake again. No way. Not me. Go find another sucker, cuz this sucker is done!

# SUICIDE

Male/Female
Dramatic
2 minutes   By Joyce Storey

Suicide among young people is at a 50-year high. A 50-year high! That is messed up! We live in one of the richest countries in the world, we have everything we could ever want at our fingertips and our generation is either killing other people or killing themselves. Is this the legacy we want to create? We are in a full-blown mental health crisis! Everybody's filling up terabytes of space on social media but nobody's talking to each other and no one's *doing* anything about it. Dominick was a great guy. He was quiet and sweet and I don't know, *human*. I had no idea... He just bottled everything up. And here we are. Some people say suicide's a sin. Well, the only sin I see is the loss of a beautiful light in the world. We did this to him. All of us, collectively. He was bullied online. And for what? Because he was sweet and kind and introverted and thoughtful? We let him down. We weren't there for him when he needed a helping hand. We're all so busy posting stuff showing how cool we are and what a fabulous life we're having and how popular we are. Well, I'm not feeling cool or fabulous or any of that. I'm angry and sad and frustrated and... I feel guilty. I should have seen the signs. Something. Doesn't anybody care about anyone else these days? Are we all so self-absorbed we can't reach out a helping hand? Actually engage with each other? Check in and make sure we're all okay? If we don't, we're just going to keep showing up in places like this and saying goodbye. And I, for one, am tired of it. I miss you Dominick. I hope you've found peace, my friend.

# TENNIS PSYCH

Male/Female
Dramatic
2 minutes    By Talia Pura

Okay, I will return this serve. I can do this. I'M READY.
(*jumps out of the way of an imaginary ball*). ARGG!
I WASN'T READY. You have to wait a second after
somebody says they're ready. How can I be ready when
I'm still talking? GIVE ME A SECOND, PLEASE. Okay, now
I'm ready. (*swings at  ball*) OOPS! SORRY. Oh, that was so
lame. YES, I AM TRYING TO REMEMBER EVERYTHING
YOU SHOWED ME. How was I supposed to absorb
any of that? This was a bad idea. I look like an idiot.
What kind of mother gives her daughter tennis lessons
for her birthday? I can't play tennis! "That's why I'm
giving you lessons," she says. "You'll learn." This is so
embarrassing. YES, GET SOME WATER. By all means…
NO, I'M FINE, THANKS. Will this hour never end? Oh no.
It can't be. Not Jamie Pringle. Look what she is wearing!
I'll bet she plays really well, too. Please, don't see me.
Just keep walking, keep… OH, HI JAMIE. YEAH, GREAT
DAY FOR TENNIS. SEE YOU. Could this day be any more
humiliating? No one else is playing in gym shorts. I want
to die. Now. Please. YES, SURE. READY WHENEVER YOU
ARE. Please, God. Lightning, heart attack, anything, just
get me out of here. (*swings at ball*) Oh, I hit it! I hit the
ball! (*swings again*). WAHOO!! I can't believe it. Two in a
row! (*swings backhand*) YEAH! Unbelievable! And with
my backhand yet. Three. I returned three shots — what?
He actually missed my shot. That isn't possible. Bring it
on, big guy. WHAT? Are you sure? That didn't feel like
anything close to an hour. YES, (*instructor comes closer*)
of course, see you next week. Can't wait!

# TIME TO GO

Male/Female
Comedic
2 minutes   By Talia Pura

Hey, do you have the time? I know that's weird. Who ever asks that anymore, right? It used to be the best line in the world. "My watch broke and I see you are wearing one." But who wears a watch anymore? I don't even own one. Our phones just do it all, I know, but I dropped mine this morning, and that finally finished it off. It's survived a lot of things, but that trip down the stairs of the subway station on my way over here was just too much. It might have made it through that, but the guy who stepped on it at the bottom of the stairs was huge! There's no coming back from that. I just have to hope that some tech genius can get all the data off of it. Sure, it's crushed, but maybe not all the way through. I thought it was finished when I dropped it in the toilet last month. But that thing with the rice really works. I was amazed. Of course, it barely spent any time in the toilet at all — hardly even got wet. You do not want to hear that story. Then there was the time my dog grabbed it when we were in the park and took off. He finally dropped it – in a storm grate. Fortunately, it hadn't rained in a while, so it was just a matter of fishing it out. Yeah, okay, right, not that interesting a story either. Ah, do you come here a lot? I do, and I don't think I've seen you here before. It's a great place, isn't it? Good coffee. Okay, decent coffee, but the Wi-Fi is fast. Not that I can use it today anyway, but — what? It's 2:30? I am so late — thanks! Thanks so much!

# TONY'S

Male
Comedic
1 minute   By Talia Pura

Don't take me back to Tony's! I can't go back to Tony's. He'll kill me. He said if I ever showed my face there again, I'd be taking my last breath. I know that sounds drastic, but he feels very strongly about his pastrami on rye. When I told him I'd tasted better, he nearly clipped me. What? It was a little dry. Come on, you didn't think it was dry? It was a little dry. Tony shouldn't have been so sensitive. If you can't take the heat, get out of the kitchen. Am I right? You know I'm right. He shouldn't have asked. I never learned to lie. Now, don't look at me like that. I have never lied to you. Never. Okay, maybe once. You asked if that dress made your ass look big. You remember, huh? Now bring that ass over here, and we can go anywhere you like. But not to Tony's, okay?

# TOO HAPPY

Male
Comedic
2 minutes   By Talia Pura

Oh wow, Brianna is absolutely, totally, the best thing that has ever happened to me. She's beautiful, she's smart, and I love everything about her. And, here's where it gets really nuts. She loves everything about me. I know, crazy, right? We tell each other every day that we are so lucky to have found each other, and we'll be together for the rest of our lives. Oh man, that is so fucked up! What am I going to do? You know that anything too good to be true is, right? I mean, how could anything possibly be this perfect? It can't, right? Good shit like this just doesn't happen to me. It doesn't happen to anybody. I mean, when was the last time that you felt as great as I do right now? Never, right? I am dead meat. I'm going to mess this up! I know I am. I've never caught her rolling her eyes at any of my dumb jokes, though — and you know there are a lot of them. She thinks I'm funny. That can't last, right? But, she gets me, and when she smiles it's like watching the most amazing sunrise on the first morning of the world. Her eyes light up and then her whole face bursts into this beautiful, endless smile. I want to die in that smile. She really is the best thing that ever happened to me, and I'm scared, you know? Is that normal? Is it normal to be freaked out about being too happy? Why can't I just relax and enjoy it? When will I stop feeling so vulnerable? When is that lump in my throat every time I think of her going to go away? I have never felt this shitty, or this wonderful, in my whole, entire life. I am the luckiest man alive!

# UNZENNING MY ZEN

Female
Comedic
2 minutes    By Joyce Storey

What the hell was that?! He said take a *normal* breath. *Nor-mal.* Not a raging, whooping gasp for your last dying breath on this earth! Honestly, you sound like a cow in heat! Do cows go into heat? Maybe that's just cats. Whatever. You are definitely in the cow category. Cats could NEVER make a sound like that. The dancing hyenas from *The Lion King* don't make as much racket as you!  We're all supposed to be having a zen moment here. And you're definitely un-zenning my zen. You get me? My mojo ain't jo-ing cuz o' you. Isn't it the first rule of yoga that we get all chillaxed and shit while communing as one? Stretching our supple, fat bodies into pretzel-like positions that we swear are good for us? Well, I've been pretzeling for half an hour here and you and your wailing are pushing me to the edge. I mean the very *edge.* And believe me, sister, when I tell you, you do *not* want to do that. For your own protection. I have anger management issues. Serious issues, ya know? Like my head could explode at any minute. I'm only here cuz my shrink said it would be good therapy for me and so far, I'm not feelin' the love. I've been downward-facing dogging for about a century now and my abs are falling off, my boobs are sagging, my muscles are burning, and my damn ears are ringing from enduring your irritating-as-hell shrieking in my ear. So, how about I chill without you practically going into labor behind me, huh? Cuz my downward-facing dog is gonna turn into a pit bull any second and I can't guarantee you'll have a face when he's done. *Capiche*?

# WORD ANGST

Male/Female
Comedic
2 minutes    By Talia Pura

You know how there are words you just can't stand to hear? No? Really? There are no words in the English language that you can't tolerate the sound of? Seriously? How is that possible? Ugh. I have a lot of them. Some aren't actually English, though. Like, angst. I *hate* how people who don't speak German like to use the word "angst" all the time, but they pronounce it ANGST, like they were starting to say the name Angie and aborted at the last minute. It's a short A that starts the word, not a long A. Drives me nuts. But not as much as the word moist. I absolutely hate the word moist. I don't like to hear it, and I especially don't like to say it out loud. You can just feel the moss dripping from the trees, slime oozing from an overripe cantaloupe, seaweed clinging to the side of a boat. MOIST. It makes my flesh crawl. So just don't use it, you tell me? Ha, easy for you to say. You don't work in my restaurant. We have an actual script that must be followed for all the dinner entrees, and yes, you guessed it — the word moist is in more than half of them. The steak is moist, the roast is moist — gawd, who wants to eat *anything* described as moist? I can't stand saying that word 50 times a night. I will go mad. Honestly, I am looking for a new job. There must be some place I can work that features food that is meant to be served dry, not — *moist*. Mexican, maybe? Surely tacos aren't moist. Japanese? One can't describe tempura as moist, can one? I don't know. All I know is, I've got to get out of this steakhouse!

# WORK FRIDGE

Male/Female
Comedic
1.5 minutes   By Talia Pura

Okay, who took it? It was right there! I swear, I am never putting my lunch in this fridge again. If you can't trust your co-workers, who can you trust? Actually, I don't trust them. Never mind the asshole who just stole my lunch — I don't trust any of them. How did I end up in this place? Go to college, they told me. You'll get a better job, they said. Right. A better job. But no one told me that it would be a better job that I'd absolutely hate! Two years I've been behind that desk in this hideous office, doing a mind-numbing job that makes me want to scream. And then, just when I think I've at least got last night's leftover lasagna to look forward to, someone steals my lunch. That is it! The proverbial last straw, breaking this camel's back. I am going back to my desk, on an empty stomach, and writing out my letter of resignation. Do you hear that? I hate all of you! I — oh, wait a minute — I forgot that I used a brown paper bag for today's lunch. It's, ah, it's right here, on the shelf, where I put it. Fine, okay, fine. So, I'll eat my lasagna and get back to work.

# WRONG PLACE

Male/Female
Dramatic
2 minutes   By Talia Pura

I am so sorry I'm late. Okay, yes, I know, I am very late. But I have a good reason. I was almost here, when I had to turn around, go back home and change my clothes. I was a mess — drenched with water and covered in mud from head to toe. No kidding, completely covered! Okay, kidding, not *completely* covered, but it was really, really bad. Obviously, I couldn't meet you looking like that. It was so embarrassing. I stopped and looked around to see if anyone else had noticed. Well, you don't want to look like an idiot, do you? (*beat*) I spend too much time looking like an idiot. (*beat)* I also spend too much time worrying about whether or not I look like an idiot. I know what you are going to say. Everyone is so worried that they may be making fools of themselves that no one is looking at me. They are all too busy looking at themselves. Yeah, yeah, I know, but believe me, this was different. I was standing there covered in mud. Obviously, people were looking at me. Everyone except the truck driver who splashed me. He was long gone. He didn't even stick around to laugh. But just before it happened, I saw the sneer, the little glint in his eye. It's true; I did. I know that it all happened in an instant, but I know that he did it on purpose. He saw that puddle, he saw me, and he just went for it. Who does that? What a masochist. (*beat*) I mean sadist. Obviously, I meant sadist. I did not step up beside that puddle on purpose. I was just in the wrong place at the wrong time. (*beat*) That's the story of my life.

# YOU SUCK

Male
Dramatic
2 minutes   By Joyce Storey

Your behavior during the interview was abominable and you are banned from any future employment with this company. Do you understand? It means you suck, bro. It's written right here in black-and-white. How could you screw this up so bad? It was a piece o' cake. It was a box job. A freaking box job. All you had to do was fold the pizza boxes and you couldn't even get *that* right. I told you to practice. But you didn't listen. You never listen. You just had to keep your mouth shut and your head down and they woulda hired you. But no. Not you. You had to go shootin' your mouth off and screw things up. I got you that interview. I stuck my neck out for you. My whole reputation was on the line and you blew it. But you didn't just blow it — you blew it up like outta the park, off the planet, into the stratosphere blew it up. You could screw up a wet dream. That is the last and I mean the *last* time I stick out my neck for you. Now I got to do the cleanup. I still got to show up for work on Monday. What happened to you? You been my best friend since we were six. You taught me how to ride a bike. You were my hero. All I wanted to do was follow you around. Everyone thought you were the coolest of cools. And now look at you. You are a used-up mess. You're not just on a downward spiral. You are on the bottom. Do you hear me? Rock-bottom. Can't you even recognize that? You're an inch from homeless. No more crashing on my couch. My girlfriend is so over you and soon she'll be over me so you got to go, dude. Clean yourself up. You're a hot mess.

# MEET THE AUTHORS

## JOYCE STOREY

Joyce Storey is an award-winning writer, producer, and actor. She is thrilled to work with Talia again on their second monologue book. They also co-authored *75 Monologues Kids Will Love!*, available at Amazon.com. Joyce's plays *Caged* and *Time Wars* have been produced in New York City. Other plays include: *The Best That Mother Knows* and *Dirty Laundry*. Screenplays include: *Guardian Angel, Blind Allie, Run Away Forever, Enchanted Forrest,* and *Thirty G's*. Her films have won awards both nationally and internationally. She has written for such publications as: *The Guardian, Front of House Magazine, Live Sound International*, and *PLSN Magazine*. Her column, *Joyce Of The Theatre*, has been read by more than 40,000 subscribers. She has written travel videos and audio tours for the *Your Guide Around* series, including: *Your Guide Around NYC, The Empire State Building, Times Square*, and *Prince Edward Island*. Her work has been published internationally in such anthologies as: *Holding Onto Forever* and *Pearls Of The Past*. Her poetry has been chosen for publication in the International Library of Poetry's *The Best Poems and Poets*. She has several projects in development, including a new musical as well two novels. She holds a bachelor's degree from Acadia University, a Producer's Certificate from Dov Simens Film School, and a Filmmaker's Certificate from the Digital Film Academy in New York. Joyce is the founder of MonologuesToGo.com and is a proud member of the Dramatists Guild and SAG-AFTRA. She is a recipient of the Terry Fox Humanitarian Award and is cited in the Marquis *Who's Who of American Women*. Joyce resides in New York City.

# TALIA PURA

Talia Pura is a playwright, actor, director, filmmaker, designer, aerial dancer and educator. She has written/produced/directed 10 short dramatic films, which have been screened at various film festivals around the world, with some licensed for television broadcasts on the Canadian Broadcasting Corporation (CBC). As a playwright, Talia has written more than 30 plays, resulting in many productions, publications, and a CBC radio commission. *Cry After Midnight*, based on her experiences as a Canadian Forces war artist in Afghanistan, represented Canada at the Women Playwrights International Conference (WPIC) in Stockholm and was read at the Canadian War Museum in Ottawa. She performed her solo drama, *This I Have Believed*, at the WPIC in Cape Town in 2015. She has also staged many of her other solo dramas, including *Confessions of an Art School Model*, which toured extensively, including a run at the New York Fringe Festival. Her book, *STAGES: Creative Ideas For Teaching Drama* was published by J. Gordon Shillingford Publishing, Inc., along with *CUES: Theatre Training and Projects from Classroom to Stage*. Her children's book, *Alexia Wants to Fly*, was published in 2015. Talia has appeared in many feature films, television shows and independent shorts. Highlights include her work with Guy Maddin in *The Saddest Music in the World* and *Sombra Dolorosa*. As a theatrical costume and set designer, she is partial to period pieces. Her aerial dance on silks includes solos with everything from symphony orchestras to rock bands, and a film commission from the 2010 Vancouver Olympic Games. After teaching high school drama for many years, she spent 15 years teaching theater at the Department of Education at the University of Winnipeg. She has enjoyed leading workshops in her own brand of devised theater in Canada, the U.S., Thailand, the Philippines, South Africa, and Brazil. Talia holds a Masters of Arts in creative writing from the University of Manitoba. Talia is the artistic director of Blue Raven Theatre, an independent theatre company dedicated to works by and about women. She is also the president of Theatre Santa Fe, the umbrella organization of the producing theatre companies of Santa Fe, the ambassador for the New Mexico region of the Dramatists Guild and a board member for the local branch of the SAG-AFTRA union. She lives in Santa Fe, New Mexico, with her visual artist/composer husband, William Pura and grandson, Oliver. (www.taliapura.com)

# NOTES